Rescue on NIM'S ISLAND

WENDY ORR

PICTURES BY GEOFF KELLY

ALLEN&UNWIN

SYDNEY • MELBOURNE • AUCKLAND • LONDON

First published in 2014

Allen & Unwin
83 Alexander Street
Crows Nest NSW 2065
Australia
Phone: (61 2) 8425 0100
Email: info@allenandunwin.com
Web: www.allenandunwin.com

A Cataloguing-in-Publication entry is available
from the National Library of Australia
www.trove.nla.gov.au

ISBN 978 1 74331 678 8

Cover and text illustrations by Geoff Kelly
Cover and text design by Sandra Nobes
Hand lettering of title by Geoff Kelly
Set in 11.5 pt Minion by Sandra Nobes

This book was printed in July 2014 at Griffin Press,
168 Cross Keys Road, Salisbury South, SA 5106.
www.griffinpress.com.au

3 5 7 9 10 8 6 4

15 AUG 2019

BNPAU

Please return/renew this item by the last date shown on this label, or on your self-service receipt.

To renew this item, visit **www.librarieswest.org.uk** or contact your library.

Your Borrower Number and PIN are required.

With thanks to Sue,
who edits with passion and wisdom,
fun and friendship.

W.O.

Coral Reef

Sandy Beach
with Coconuts

Black Rocks

Keyhole Cove

Hissing
Stones

Sea Lion Point

Selkie's Rock

Camp

Shell Beach

Lookout
Palm

Turtle
Beach

Nim's Is'Land

Chapter 1

From: Nim@RusoeSanctuaryforRare&EndangeredSpecies.com
To: Edmund@kidmail.com
Date: Monday, 12 May, 5:45pm
Subject: Invaders!

Hi Edmund

The island is going to be invaded again! Jack's inviting four other scientists here for a conference on turning algae into biofuel. I can hardly believe it. I know how much he loves plankton and algae – but we've spent our whole lives trying to keep our home secret. He says it'll be okay because the World Organisation of Scientists will choose who gets to come, so they'll be people who understand how special this place is.

Nim – as confused as Fred sleeping on Selkie's back and ending up at sea

P.S. They won't even have to run away from home like the last invader...

From: Edmund@kidmail.com

To: Nim@RusoeSanctuaryforRare&EndangeredSpecies.com

Date: Monday, 12 May, 4:55pm

Subject: re: Invaders!

And they probably won't get grounded when they get home.

But maybe they need an assistant? Someone who wants to be a scientist when he grows up, who already knows you and Selkie and Fred and Jack, and has already helped conduct important scientific research on the island?

Edmund – as green as a tree frog with envy

From: Nim@RusoeSanctuaryforRare&EndangeredSpecies.
com

To: Edmund@kidmail.com

Date: Monday, 12 May, 5:58pm

Subject: Are you still grounded?

From: Edmund@kidmail.com

To: Nim@RusoeSanctuaryforRare&EndangeredSpecies.com

Date: Monday, 12 May, 4:59pm

Subject: Grounding officially finishes June 30.

When is the conference? Have you got a plan?

From: Nim@RusoeSanctuaryforRare&EndangeredSpecies.
com

To: Edmund@kidmail.com

Date: Monday, 12 May, 8:12pm

Subject: My plan is useless

The conference is Monday, 23 June. And Jack says the
World Organisation of Scientists won't accept research
done by kids so we can't be assistants. And they've
already chosen the scientists so he can't change the date.
AND he'll send you right back if you run away again.

Nim – as mad as a hermit crab who's lost her shell

From: Edmund@kidmail.com
To: Nim@RusoeSanctuaryforRare&EndangeredSpecies.com
Date: Monday, 12 May, 7:13pm
Subject: It was worth a try

Edmund – as crushed as a shell-less hermit crab
underneath Selkie

From: Edmund@kidmail.com
To: Nim@RusoeSanctuaryforRare&EndangeredSpecies.com
Date: Tuesday, 13 May, 4:30pm
Subject: Negotiations

If I wash the dishes every night, take out the garbage,
keep my bedroom clean AND babysit the twins downstairs
– the naughtiest kids in the whole world – for the next two
Saturdays, I'm ungrounded on Sunday the 22nd June.

Edmund – rushing to clean my bedroom, just in case

From: Nim@RusoeSanctuaryforRare&EndangeredSpecies.com
To: Edmund@kidmail.com
Date: Tuesday, 13 May, 5:35pm
Subject: Yay for ungrounding

But I still haven't got a plan.

I've never met any twins. I think it would be fun.
How do you sit on them both at the same time? Maybe
Selkie could help you. Ha ha! (I know that's not what
babysitting means! I've read books about it.)

Nim – laughing about Selkie babysitting the naughty
kids

4

From: Edmund@kidmail.com

To: Nim@RusoeSanctuaryforRare&EndangeredSpecies.com

Date: Tuesday, 13 May, 4:37pm

Subject: Selkie babysitting

I'd like to see that.

From: Nim@RusoeSanctuaryforRare&EndangeredSpecies.com

To: Edmund@kidmail.com

Date: Friday, 16 May, 10:11am

Subject: Cross your fingers

Jack got an email yesterday about the scientists who are coming. Two of them are married to each other and they want to bring their children. The other two work at a university in Brisbane but they aren't married to each other and neither of them have kids. The family scientists have a boat so they're going to sail it here and pick up the others on the way.

So I told Jack if other kids were coming that you should too, because you know all about babysitting, and we don't know how old these kids are. This morning he FINALLY said he's going to email your parents and the Brisbane scientists and ask if you can come with them!!!!

Nim – as excited as Fred with a smashed-open coconut

Chapter 2

IN A PALM TREE, on an island, in the middle of the wide blue sea, was a girl.

Nim's hair was wild, her eyes were bright, and around her neck she wore three cords. One was for a spyglass, one for a whirly, whistling shell and the other a fat, red pocketknife in a sheath.

With the spyglass at her eye, she watched the boat chug closer. It was a wooden fishing boat with a green-painted cabin; it was solid enough to cross the deeper dark ocean but small enough to weave through the maze of reef protecting the island. The people on the deck were waving and pointing. Nim's stomach tumbled like a coconut falling from a tree, and she didn't know if it was excited-tumbling or scared, or maybe just not-quite-believing. For three days and three nights, strangers were going to be on the island. Seven strangers – and one friend.

She whistled her shell, three short, sharp notes that carried up to the lab in the rainforest where her father was working. Sometimes Jack was so busy studying his plankton or researching his algae that he forgot to listen. But he whistled back right away: one-two-three, and a moment later he was zipping down the hill on the flying fox.

He let go of the rope and skidded onto the sand below Nim's tree.

'Are you ready?' he called.

'No,' Nim called back. In all those months she'd been waiting to see Edmund again, she hadn't imagined meeting him in front of so many people.

But Selkie was lolloping across the beach, barking deep, anxious sea lion grunts about a new boat coming in to their island. Nim couldn't let Selkie face the strangers alone.

'Come on, Fred!' she said.

Fred was an iguana, spiky as a dragon, with a cheerful snub nose. He clung tightly to Nim's shoulder as she slid down the tree.

The motor's chugging stopped. The boat rocked gently in the silence. A cheerful-looking man with dark skin and a red T-shirt was standing in the bow, at the very front of the boat. He bent to drop the anchor over the side, and Nim heard the rattle of the chain as it settled onto the sandy ocean floor.

Together, Nim and Fred, Jack and Selkie headed across the beach to meet their visitors.

EDMUND WAS ON the deck. He waved to Nim, but looked as if he didn't know what to do next. Behind him were a

8

tall, slim woman, pale as a lily, and an even taller, thinner and paler man. They stayed in the cockpit as the man in the red T-shirt returned to the stern of the boat, unclipped the rubber dinghy hanging on the back rail, and lowered it to the water.

He climbed in and picked up the oars. 'Who's first ashore?'

The tall couple stepped over the railing and down to the dinghy.

'Go ahead, Edmund,' a blonde woman called from the wheelhouse. 'I've got to sign off the logbook.'

'Thanks!' said Edmund, and he said it again as the dinghy's rubber bottom touched the sand a few minutes later. He was back in his favourite place in the world – he could hardly believe he was here.

He splashed in through the sparkling blue water. He had a pack on his back and his shoes in his hand, and he was looking all around him, drinking in every detail that he might have forgotten.

The tall couple took off their shoes and waded in after him, and the man in the red T-shirt rowed back to the boat for his family.

The blonde woman came out of the wheelhouse holding a toddler by the hand. The little boy squealed with excitement as she lowered him into his father's waiting arms.

'Tiffany and Tristan!' she called. 'Time to go ashore.'

A boy and girl came out from the cabin. They were

the same height and had the same dark hair and wary expressions as they climbed down to the dinghy after their mother.

They're twins! thought Nim. *Like the naughty kids Edmund babysits. Except they're our age, and they'll be nice.* Suddenly the scared part of her excitement evaporated into the clear blue sky. Her friend was here, and two new friends as well. She ran the rest of the way across the beach to meet them.

UNTIL A YEAR ago, Nim had never wanted any friends except Selkie, Fred and the other animals. She'd lived alone on the island with her father for as long as she could remember, until Alex Rover, the most famous adventure writer in the world, had come to rescue her when Jack was lost at sea. In the end Nim had to rescue Alex, but when Jack came home, Alex decided to stay. Now Alex was part of the family and Nim didn't want her to ever leave again. But she'd still never thought she needed friends who were kids like her, and could talk with words instead of iguana sneezes and sea lion whuffles.

That was until the Troppo Tourist cruise ship had sealnapped Selkie. Nim had stowed away to steal her back again, and met Ben and Erin on the ship. When it was time to say goodbye, they were all so sad that Jack said her new friends could visit the next summer. Nim knew that they'd love the island and that she'd love showing it to them. But Erin and Ben hadn't been able to come after all. Their parents had said that the family couldn't afford to travel so far again.

For the first time in her life, Nim was lonely. She swam with Selkie and explored with Fred; she had school with Jack and read Alex's books – but sometimes she wished she had someone else to do things with.

And then one day a boy had arrived. Edmund had been saving and scheming ever since he'd seen the island from the Troppo Tourist cruise ship. He'd run away from home, jumped off a fishing boat with his rubber dinghy, and rowed all the way to Shell Beach in the middle of the night. Nim had been suspicious at first but by the time Jack sailed Edmund home again, they'd had adventures, proved that the island was an international sanctuary for rare and endangered species, and turned into friends.

That was six months ago.

Now Edmund was back on the island, and part of Nim wanted to leap and shriek like an excited monkey. The other part couldn't remember how to talk to real people who were outside the computer.

Edmund looked as if he couldn't remember how either.

The tall couple could. They were both smooth and elegant, polished as sea glass. On a gold chain around her neck, the woman wore a chunk of gleaming yellow amber with a scorpion trapped inside.

The man shook Jack's hand. 'Dr Lance Bijou,' he introduced himself, 'and my wife Dr Leonora Bijou.'

Those aren't the right names! thought Nim.

'Where are Dr Selina Ashburn and Professor Peter Hunterstone?' Jack demanded.

'Unfortunately,' said Leonora, 'they were both taken ill at the last minute.'

'We expect them to recover next week,' said Lance, 'but for now, they are too sick to travel.'

'That's terrible!' Jack exclaimed.

'Sad,' Lance agreed. 'But as my wife is a biologist and I am a geologist, we volunteered to drop everything and take their places.'

'And since they'd agreed to bring Edmund,' said Leonora, 'we felt we had to do that too.'

'That was kind,' said Jack.

Leonora nodded graciously.

Like a queen, thought Nim. She looked across at Edmund. He was too busy hugging Selkie and scratching Fred's spiky head to look back at her.

This isn't how it's supposed to be! Nim thought. Maybe Alex was right to hide from everyone. 'I don't want anyone to know I'm here,' she'd said. Because even though Alex Rover was the most famous adventure writer in the world, she was still afraid of spiders, snakes, and meeting new people. That's why only Jack and Nim were on the beach meeting the scientists.

THE DINGHY LANDED and the family splashed out, the mother carrying the toddler. The twins didn't look as if they wanted to be there. Their father pulled the dinghy up high on the beach and turned it upside down so it wouldn't fill up with rain.

'At least no one's going to steal it here!' he laughed.

The woman put the toddler down on the sand. 'I'm Anika Lowe, the coral scientist. This is my husband Ryan, the climatologist, and Ollie, Tiffany and Tristan.'

'You're looking forward to this, aren't you, Tiff-Tris?' said Ryan.

The twins didn't answer. They stared around as if they were wondering what was worth looking at, then put on their headphones and sat down, back to back on the sand.

Leonora caught Nim's eye and smiled. 'Don't worry about them,' she whispered. 'I'm very excited about being on your beautiful island!'

In fact, Nim's island was the most beautiful island in the whole world. It had white shell beaches, pale gold sand and tumbled black rocks where the spray threw rainbows into the sky. It had a fiery mountain with green rainforest on the slopes and grassland at the bottom. There was a pool of fresh water to drink and a slippery waterfall to slide down.

There used to be a hut in a hidden hollow of the grasslands, but when it blew away, they built a new house higher up the hill. It was tucked deep in the rainforest, close to the freshwater pool, and the corner of two walls joined the trunk of the most magnificent tree in the forest. The tree was so tall that no matter how far Nim tilted her

head back to see the top, she couldn't see where the tree ended and the sky began. Its oldest roots were solid grey walls higher than Nim, and its youngest roots were vines dangling from the trunk. Nim liked to sit in its branches and imagine the stories it could tell about the animals it had seen, from the tiniest creeping insect to Galileo the great-winged frigate bird skimming overhead.

Jack said the tree was so old it could have seen Chica's great-great-grandmother laying her eggs on the beach. Chica was a sea turtle, and they can live for a hundred years, so it was a long time since her great-grandmother had hatched and crawled to the sea.

Alex thought it had even seen dinosaurs playing when it was young; but Alex was better at imagining than science.

Nim just knew that it was a tree full of stories, and soon it would have a new one about the people coming here for Jack's conference. Maybe it would be a story that could save the world.

'We need a new fuel that can run any kind of motor without polluting the earth or sky or sea. I think algae are the answer – and if we get different scientists together, with different ways of looking at the problem, maybe we'll come up with the right question,' Jack had said. 'Sometimes the greatest discoveries in science are found by accident.'

Chapter 3

No one knew what to do first. Tiffany and Tristan went on listening to music with their eyes closed. Edmund wandered down the beach. Ryan and Anika looked all around, smiling and swinging Ollie between them.

Leonora pulled a slim bottle out of her bag. 'Coconut oil is very good for the skin,' she said to Nim, smoothing a few drops into her hands. 'Try some!'

Nim couldn't say that Alex always said so too, and that was why she'd made coconut oil for Alex's birthday last month. She held out her hands obediently.

Selkie humphed. Fred twined around Nim's feet in a prickly hug.

'Fred's right,' said Nim, 'it's time for lunch!'

The iguana skittered excitedly to her shoulder, spraying his cool salt-water sneeze against her neck.

'Yuck!' said the twins.

'Sneeze on me too,' Ollie begged.

Nim went back to the lookout palm and picked up two coconuts lying on the sand. With a rock and a spike, she punched a hole for the juice, and handed the first nut to Anika.

Anika drank from the shell, just like Nim and Jack. 'Delicious!' she said, trickling some juice into Ollie's mouth. The little boy laughed, and grabbed the coconut for more.

'Gross!' said Tristan.

'Don't you have straws?' asked Tiffany.

'No,' said Nim, starting to feel as prickly as Fred.

'It's much better like this,' said Ryan, drinking the rest of the juice.

'We only get things from the supply ship that we really need,' said Jack. He opened the other coconut and handed it to Leonora. She drank neatly, without spilling a drop.

When they were finished, Nim cracked the shells and pried out the slippery flesh. Fred snatched a piece and gulped it down. (Marine iguanas don't eat coconut, but no one had ever told Fred.)

The twins screwed up their faces.

'He's so ugly!' said Tiffany.

Selkie huffed crossly.

'Wow! I didn't know seals had such bad breath!' Tristan exclaimed.

Nim had never imagined that someone could come to her island and not like it. She'd thought the twins were going to be friends! Fury, hot as Fire Mountain, bubbled and rose inside her. She could feel the lava-words ready to explode from her mouth.

She ran down the beach, past Edmund, and dived off the rocks.

The water was cool and welcoming. Nim swam hard and fast, until the peaceful waves rocked her into calm. The funny faces of clownfish darting between fronds of coral made her smile. She rolled over and floated on her back with the warm sun on her face, drifting wherever the waves wanted her to go.

Then a great brown body shot up beneath her, tumbling her over and around until Nim was swallowing ocean, coughing and spluttering. 'I wasn't going too far!' she protested.

The sea lion kept on nudging. Nim looked out and saw that the beach was much further away than she wanted it to be.

'Sorry,' she said. 'You were right.'

Selkie snorted, and dived under again. Nim slipped onto the sea lion's back and clung tight as they glided through the waves, thumping over, ducking under. The world was the way it should be again.

Three more days, she thought. *Then the visitors will all go away and everything will be just the way it always is.*

Selkie swam back towards her favourite rock and, with a last magnificent dive and splash, tumbled Nim onto the beach.

Edmund was there. He sat so still that a cormorant was standing beside him drying its wings, as if it hadn't noticed this new human.

'You know the coolest thing about you riding Selkie?' he asked, as if he hadn't been ignoring her half an hour ago. 'She could be free – but she wants to stick around you.'

'She is free!' exclaimed Nim. 'But she's my friend – and she helped my dad look after me when I was a baby. Sometimes she forgets I'm not still a little sea lion pup.'

'Did you used to be a little sea lion pup?' asked Edmund.

Nim began to splutter, and then she laughed. They both laughed so long that Selkie got bored and swam away, and Fred scuttled across the beach towards them. He climbed to Nim's shoulder and sneezed reproachfully at her.

Edmund laughed so hard he nearly fell off the rock.

JACK AND NIM showed the scientists where to set up their camp on the grasslands near the beach. The Lowes had a big family tent for all five of them. Lance and Leonora had a tent that was nearly as big for the two of them, and Edmund had a little tent for himself.

'Will you be nervous on your own?' Anika asked him.

'We're right here if you need us,' said Ryan.

'Don't worry,' said Leonora, stroking her scorpion pendant. 'Edmund knows we're always keeping an eye on him.'

'Thanks,' said Edmund. 'But I like being by myself.'

Tiffany rolled her eyes and whispered to Tristan. Tristan laughed.

'Doesn't everyone like being by themselves?' asked Nim.

'It's a very important skill,' said Anika. 'Even if it's hard for twins to believe it.'

Nim felt more muddled than ever. It was like watching a new flock of birds: she knew that there was a game going on, but she couldn't work out the rules.

'Now,' said Leonora, 'I'd like to ask Nim to be my guide around the island. I'm sure she knows every cave and crevice.'

Jack laughed. 'She certainly does! But we'll show you around all together. When everyone's got a good idea of the island they can decide where they want to research tomorrow.'

'Of course,' said Leonora. 'I mustn't keep your clever young daughter all to myself.'

A puffer fish of pride swelled inside Nim: the beautiful biologist wanted to be her friend. Suddenly it didn't matter so much that Tiffany and Tristan didn't.

But Edmund was watching Leonora the way Fred watched a snake.

WALKING ON SHELL Beach with other people was slow and strange. The jangle of voices filled Nim's ears so she couldn't hear the cry of birds or the shushing of the sea. Her toes didn't notice the warm sand beneath them. But most of all her mind was too busy noticing what other people were doing to think her own thoughts.

Seeing Ollie riding on Ryan's shoulders made her remember the safe excitement of riding on Jack's. But when the little boy climbed higher to stand, wobbling dangerously as he grabbed his father's head with one hand and pointed at a leaping dolphin with the other, Nim felt sad. She wished she could remember far enough back to hear her own mum saying, 'Careful!' and pulling her back to safety, the way that Anika was.

'Is it just you and Jack on the island?' Leonora asked, as if she was reading Nim's mind.

And Alex Rover, Nim nearly said, because the biologist's voice sounded so kind that it was hard to lie.

'For a long time,' she said at last.

'What about your mother?' asked Lance.

His voice was silky smooth too, and Nim didn't know why she really didn't want to tell them about her mum.

Nim couldn't remember her mother very well, but every morning she said hello to her picture. In the photograph, her mum looked happy-excited, because it was the day she went diving with a blue whale to investigate exactly what he was eating. Jack always said the experiment would have been all right, it should have been safe, except that the Troppo Tourists came in their huge pink-and-purple boat, racing around the whale and bumping its nose. The whale panicked and dived, so deep that no one ever knew where or when he came back up again.

Nim's mother never came back up at all.

'She died when I was a baby,' said Nim, and Leonora laid a smooth, slim-fingered hand on her shoulder in sympathy.

Nim wasn't used to other people touching her, even if they meant to be kind. The hairs on her arms prickled till she was as spiky as Fred. Behind her, Selkie barked twice. Nim rushed back and threw her arms around the sea lion's warm neck. 'Everything's okay,' she whispered, but Selkie whuffled and sniffed her as if Nim had been doing something dangerous.

'Selkie wants me to walk with her,' Nim called, as Jack led everyone up the point to Turtle Beach.

Selkie snorted yes.

Edmund was watching. He'd been walking a little way off from everyone else, not talking. 'I'd forgotten how smart she was,' he said.

Selkie looked at him and barked.

'She wants you to walk with us,' Nim interpreted.

'Except she doesn't really walk,' said Edmund.

'She galumphs,' said Nim.

'I've never met anyone else who galumphs,' said Edmund. 'It's sad: Dr Ashburn told me that even though she's working with algae now, sea lions are the reason she became a biologist. She was nearly as excited as me about coming here.'

'And then she got so sick.'

Edmund nodded. 'She was okay last night when she phoned to tell me what time to meet. She was going out to celebrate with Professor Hunterstone and some scientist friends. It's weird that they both got so sick afterwards.'

'Tragic,' said Lance, popping up from behind a tussock.

SELKIE DECIDED SHE'D had enough galumphing and slid back to the water. Every once in a while Nim saw her sleek dark head poking through the waves, keeping watch until the people were out of sight. A little while later she was waiting for them on the other side of the island.

Jack led the visitors wide around the rainforest to cross the mountain.

Nim was glad he'd chosen that trail, even though the ground was gravelly and black and the plants were grey spikes. Their house, his lab, and Alex Rover's writing studio were hidden deep in the rainforest, and she didn't want Tiffany and Tristan to be anywhere near her home.

Tiff-Tris, their dad had called them. It made them sound smaller and cuter than they were: more like their little brother Ollie. He'd walked a long way along the cliffs by himself, but now Ryan was piggybacking him again, stepping carefully over the skidding, loose stones.

From the curve of the mountain, sometimes all they could see was the dense green rainforest. Other times there were gaps and they could see over the island and far out to sea. Edmund took picture after picture. Once they stopped to look down at a waterfall gushing from steep grey cliffs.

'It looks different from up here,' said Edmund, when he'd taken twenty pictures of the waterfall, the pond that it splashed into, the rock bridge that arched across the pond, and a few more of the cliffs.

Nim laughed. 'It's much prettier when you're not falling into it!'

Tristan looked at them curiously, but they didn't explain. 'What's that?' he asked, pointing to a hollow on the bare hill, not far below them. 'It looks like the start of a tunnel.'

'A water-tunnel,' said Nim. 'If it rains a lot, a waterfall comes out of it and runs into the big one on the cliffs.'

'It better not rain while we're here,' sniffed Tiffany.

A short walk later they were on top of a hill of black boulders that tumbled down to a wilder sea. White-foamed waves sprayed rainbows as they crashed onto the rocks. The visitors gasped, and crept carefully down the trail with their backs to the hill. Jack was leading the way; Nim stayed at the rear to make sure no one slipped behind.

She had never walked so slowly, with so many stops. She'd never stood still in front of one of the shrubby trees growing out of the hill on the edge of the path. That was probably why she'd never felt the cold breeze coming out from behind it.

Nim knew every trail and every mood of her island. That's what she thought. She knew that the breeze from the sea was cooler and fresher than the warm air, heavy with the scent of plants, wafting across the rainforest. She knew that the sun shining on the rocks warmed the air in front of them.

She absolutely knew that she should not be feeling a cold wind on her back. She ducked behind the tree.

In the rocky side of the hill, just waiting for her to find it, was a big-enough-to-climb-through hole. Nim stuck her head into the darkness. She could feel the emptiness and the cool, dank wind that blew through it.

It was like finding an egg from a bird she'd never seen before: a surprise gift from the island.

Nim had discovered a new cave.

Chapter 4

IF JACK HAD been right in front of her, Nim would have called out. She might have even if it had been Leonora. But Tiffany was the last in the line before her, so Nim didn't say anything. What if she was wrong, and this was only a hole in the rock, not a real cave? She had to know what it was before she could share it.

There wasn't time for that now.

She rushed to catch up. The visitors were so nervous of falling off the narrow cliff path that they hadn't even noticed she'd dropped behind.

'This is what we've come to see!' Jack announced, at the entrance to the Emergency Cave. Everyone followed him in except Tiffany. She stayed outside with her back pressed to the cliff wall, staring anxiously down at the sea.

She's acting like there's something to be scared of in the cave! Nim thought indignantly.

The Emergency Cave used to be where they bunkered down during house-wrecking storms, but now it doubled as Jack's how-do-algae-grow-in-the-cold laboratory. He still did experiments in his lab behind the house, but to find algae that could be a fuel, he needed to know how fast they could grow when they were cold. So as well as ropes, torches, and cans of emergency food like rice pudding and baked beans, the cave held rows of test tubes and Petri dishes.

'Fascinating!' said Leonora, studying a tube full of shimmering algae.

Nim glowed brighter too, knowing that all these scientists had come to see Jack's research, and that somehow, this meeting might change the world. She stayed happy the whole walk back to the camp, even when Tristan made vomiting noises at the rotten-egg smell from the Hissing Stones and Tiffany stole a yellow flower off a bowerbird's nest.

THAT NIGHT EVERYONE collected driftwood from the beaches and sticks from the forest to make a giant bonfire on the sand. They roasted sweet potatoes from Nim and Jack's garden, and toasted marshmallows that Anika had brought from the city.

Nim's marshmallow caught on fire. She blew it out fast. She'd never had a marshmallow before, and she didn't want it all burned up before she'd tasted it.

'That's my favourite way too,' said Edmund, poking his stick into the fire till the marshmallow was flaming bright. He blew it out, pulled off the ashy cover, and sucked the melting white mess off his stick.

Nim tried, and he was right. She still liked sweet potatoes better, but flaming marshmallows were more exciting.

After dinner, the adults pulled their fold-out chairs closer around the campfire and talked science talk. Jack told them about the experiments he was doing with algae.

'We need to find a fuel that doesn't destroy land or oceans, and doesn't use up crops that people need for food. Algae grow fast, and some of them produce oil. But the ones I've found that grow fast don't make oil, and the ones that produce oil don't grow fast. I'm hoping that with all of us working together, we'll find the answer to how they can do both.

'It was a big decision to invite you,' he continued, 'because Nim and I have worked very hard to keep our island secret. The ancestors of its plants and animals have lived here for thousands and even millions of years, and we want to make sure that they always stay safe in their own environment. But the island is part of the world, and right now we need to work together for the whole world's environment to become safer.'

Everyone smiled and clapped, then Lance gave a speech about how honoured they were to come here, and about being part of the world family of scientists, and how he hoped that everyone here respected the island as much as he did. It was quite a long speech, and Nim closed her eyes as she rested her head against Selkie's warm back. She barely even heard Anika talking about seaweeds and kelp, the biggest algae of all, or Ryan discussing why it was important to know exactly where the ocean's temperatures were changing most, and what happened to the algae that grew there.

But she woke up when Leonora began to speak, because the elegant biologist made her science into a story. Even little Ollie sat quietly to listen.

'Algae were the first form of life,' said Leonora. 'Learning about their history will give us clues about the algae we have now.' Then she told them about the fossils she'd found in different places around the world: dinosaur bones and footprints, fern leaves and seashells.

'Like your necklace?' asked Tiffany.

The amber scorpion had its head raised and its pincers spread. In the flickering firelight, it looked as if it was still angry and struggling to get out.

'My lovely little friend, caught in tree sap millions of years ago, but still perfect and fierce,' said Leonora, stroking the stone.

Tiffany shuddered.

'It's not their fault they're poisonous,' Leonora said severely. 'I'm like Nim: I love all creatures, whether they're ugly or beautiful. That's why I'm a biologist.'

Nim swelled with pride all over again. She forgot that a second ago she'd been shuddering with Tiffany, because she hated to think of any animal struggling and trapped.

'You see,' Leonora continued, 'even though we're studying algae now, if we find a fossil on the island, no matter how small, it could still help us on our quest.'

WHEN THE FIRE's embers died
down, Jack and Nim headed up the
trail to their house. Fred dozed on Nim's
shoulder. She hugged Selkie goodnight, so
that her friend could go down to the rocks where the king
of the sea lions was barking for her.

But Selkie hadn't let Nim out of her sight since the
scientists arrived, and she wasn't going to start now. She
galumphed up the hill with them, not caring that the trail
was narrow and littered with sticks and rocks.

'It's okay,' Nim told her, 'they're not Troppo Tourists!'

HRUMPH! Selkie snorted, so loudly that Alex came out to see what was wrong. Nim knew that meant Alex had finished writing for the day. When Alex was inside a story, a whole herd of sea lions couldn't get her out of it.

'Doesn't Selkie trust your visitors?' she asked.

'Two of the kids were rude to her,' said Nim. 'But she was happy about seeing Edmund. She even gave him a kiss when she thought I wasn't looking.'

'But Selina Ashburn, the biologist who was supposed to bring Edmund, couldn't come,' Jack told Alex. 'She and Peter Hunterstone were taken ill at the last minute, so Lance and Leonora Bijou took their place.'

'It's lucky they were the same kind of scientists,' said Nim.

'Ah,' said Alex, with a funny sort of smile.

'What does *Ah* mean?' Nim asked.

Alex laughed. 'It means I've been writing so many stories I forget that there aren't nearly as many bad guys in real life. And that sometimes amazingly lucky coincidences really do happen.'

She started stacking a sprawl of papers covered with diagrams and notes. 'Speaking of bad guys: I'm trying to work out how much time my Hero has to escape.'

'Where does he have to escape from?' Nim asked.

'A temple. The Bad Guys have set dynamite to explode it…Did you know that it takes forty-five seconds to burn thirty centimetres of dynamite fuse?'

Nim and Jack hadn't known. They were used to Alex asking questions like that.

'So I need to work out how fast my Hero can run, and multiply that by how far away he has to get from the explosion, and that'll tell me how much time he needs before the temple explodes.'

Even though she knew now that Alex Rover wasn't the hero of the books, and that everything that happened in them was made up in Alex's head, Nim still loved listening to the stories. She loved the way Alex talked about the characters as if they were friends, and she especially loved when she could help work things out.

So they talked about the Hero and the Lady Hero he was saving, and the jewel that was inside the temple, and when she went to bed Nim realised she hadn't told Alex all about the real visitors. She'd wanted to tell her about Leonora's scorpion trapped in amber, and how Leonora was as smooth and shiny as a jewel herself.

She went to sleep hearing the biologist's silky voice saying that learning about fossils could save the world. Nim was going to do everything she could to help her find something perfect.

And when she did, everyone would want to be her friend again. Even Tiffany.

Chapter 5

IT WAS STILL dark when Nim slipped her headlamp onto her forehead and tiptoed out of the house. Fred scuttled out from his rock, and Selkie slid across the porch, whuffling and snorting hello. They never cared how early it was; if Nim was doing something, they wanted to do it with her.

Fred especially loved it when Nim was wearing her headlamp, because he could do his two favourite things at the same time: riding on Nim's shoulder and catching the insects that flew into the light.

Selkie lollopped ahead. Selkie was a lot bigger than Nim, but she could move nearly as quietly, and much faster. She started down the hill as Nim filled her bamboo drinker from the waterfall.

'Wait!' Nim called. 'We're going to the cave.'

Selkie snorted a disapproving sort of *humph*. 'Not the Emergency Cave,' Nim added quickly. 'I think I've found a new one.'

Selkie *humphed* again. She didn't care which cave it was: she didn't like any of the caverns and tunnels on the cliffs above the Black Rocks.

'We'll meet you there,' said Nim.

Selkie sighed a deep, sea lion sigh, and galumphed on down the hill to the sea. Nim and Fred followed the creek deeper into the rainforest.

They passed the side-trail to Alex Rover's writing studio. Alex liked having her studio away from the house so that she had to go outside twice a day, because when she was in the middle of writing a book, she forgot about things like going for a walk, or even eating. Sometimes Nim had to go and knock on the door and remind her that it was time for dinner, just like she had to remind Jack when he was busy with science experiments.

Luckily Nim always had Selkie and Fred to remind her when it was time to eat. They never forgot.

After Alex's studio, the rocks beside the creek got bigger. The trail got skinnier and the rainforest got thicker. Vines dangled down from the trees and across the ground, ghostly and shadowed in the bobbing light of Nim's headlamp. It was hard to tell if they were vines or snakes.

Nim liked watching snakes, and she liked stroking their sun-warmed, gleaming skin, but she didn't like accidentally bumping into them. They mightn't mean to hurt, but if they were frightened and bit her, she could die anyway.

It was hard to believe that something so beautiful could kill you.

Fred believed it. Every big vine reminded him of the python that had wanted to eat him for lunch. Pythons aren't venomous, but you'll still end up dead if they swallow you. Nim had grabbed Fred just in time, and they'd both felt shivery for a long time.

He snuggled close into her neck now. Nim tickled his chin.

'Don't worry,' she said. 'I'll never let anyone hurt you.' Fred sneezed gratefully. He was glad when the blackness faded to a grey dawn light, and it was easier to see if the snakes lying across the trail were real hissing, biting ones, or just vines pretending.

Now Nim could hear the waterfall rumbling off the cliffs, and the creek rushing as the water spilled into it from the pond at the bottom.

Through the shadows, she could see the dark shape of the rock bridge arching over the pond to the cliff.

The cliff looked high from here, but it had seemed even higher when she'd climbed it with Edmund. Especially when he'd fallen off into the pond, and she'd jumped in after him. That was what they hadn't wanted to tell Tristan and Tiffany yesterday.

But falling into the pond was how they'd found the cave at the bottom of the cliff – and the bats. They were big brown fruit bats, and there was only one other colony of this species in the whole world. They were just about as rare as anything could be without being extinct.

The bats were one of the reasons that the World Organisation of Scientists had classified Nim's island as a wildlife sanctuary. It was like a circle, Nim thought: finding the bats had helped keep her island safe, because the world wanted the island to keep the bats safe.

Then the sun rose behind Fire Mountain. Nim turned off her headlamp; Fred swallowed one last bug and fell asleep on her shoulder. Pink light trickled through the trees, glinting off the waterfall, pond and creek. But Nim hurried on the other way, across the creek and around the side of the hill. It was time to find out if she really had discovered another new cave.

SELKIE WAS WAITING at the top of the Black Rocks, whuffling reproachfully.

'Sorry,' said Nim, 'but this will be worth it.'

They followed the path to the tree where she'd felt the cool breeze, and there it was: a hole in the rock, like a door into adventure. It was about as high as her waist: Nim bent and looked into the dark nothingness. She switched on her headlamp.

NO! Selkie barked, in her deepest, strongest voice, because the hole was big enough for Nim and even Jack, but not for a sea lion. Selkie didn't like Nim going where she couldn't follow.

For a moment Nim wished she'd woken Edmund up to come with her. It would have been fun to have another adventure together – and Selkie was right about how dangerous it was to go into a cave on her own. But she'd come all the way up here, she wasn't going to turn around now.

'I just want to have a look,' she said. 'I won't be long.'

She stretched further into the hole until she could touch the ground on the other side, and slid into the cave.

Except that it wasn't a cave after all, just a tunnel: she couldn't quite stand up in it.

'I thought it would be big!' she told Fred.

Fred didn't answer. Selkie stuck her head in and barked that if Nim didn't know what it was like she should come straight back out.

But Nim could already see that the tunnel got steadily wider and higher, so she crouch-walked, and then she walked standing straight, and then her headlamp was shining into the biggest cave she had ever imagined. It was

as tall as a building in Alex Rover's city and as magical as
something in one of her stories. Because it wasn't just big:
it was glimmering with light.

Nim turned her headlamp off and stared.

Strings of shimmering blue glow-worms danced from
the ceiling, their tiny lights turning rocks into jewels.
Toadstools glimmered green from the floor: fat and lumpy
or delicate and spindly, but all shining with a soft, eerie
glow. Stalactites dripped down and stalagmites grew up.
Some were as small as her little finger but the oldest were
as tall and thick as trees; in some places they'd joined to
make solid pillars from roof to ceiling. There were arches
that looked like doorways to more tunnels and mysteries,
and windows into blackness.

In the centre of the cavern, big brown fruit bats were
circling and squeaking.

What are they doing here? thought Nim.

Because they were definitely the same type of bats that lived in the cave under the Waterfall Cliffs, and they were definitely settling down here. Except they're settling *up*, she thought, watching the bats grab their favourite ceiling spots with their toes, so they could dangle upside down for a good day's sleep.

She went nearer. Each of the upside-down bats had a tiny baby bat clinging to her stomach.

'It's the nursery cave!' Nim exclaimed. She'd read lots about bats after she and Edmund had found the main colony. One of her favourite facts was that some species had a separate place for the mothers and babies until the pups were old enough to live in the main cave. Jack didn't think their bats did that, but Nim had always hoped so. She liked thinking about all those mothers and babies in a special safe place.

And here it was: the nursery for the most endangered bats in the world.

The only mystery was why she hadn't seen any flying in when she was outside the entrance. She hadn't even seen any droppings in the tunnel.

If the bats were being so careful to keep this nursery hidden, it was even more important not to disturb them. Nim tiptoed back to where she'd come in. It was easy to find because a huge stalagmite, as fat around as Selkie, stood just by the entrance to the tunnel.

Another tunnel led off to the left. It was tall enough to

39

walk in and curved like a rainbow: 'So it can't go far,' Nim told Fred, and followed it.

But the tunnel didn't go anywhere at all; around the curve it widened and ended against a wall of rock. 'We must be right next to where we came in,' said Nim. 'Can you hear us, Selkie?'

Selkie barked yes. Then in case they hadn't heard the first time, she stuck her head as far as she could into the entrance and barked again. The rumble was so loud that the end wall shook. Crumbs of limestone drifted down.

'We're just on the other side from you!' Nim shouted back, knocking hard to make sure Selkie understood. A whole flake of rock crumbled and fell.

'Oops!' said Nim.

Then she saw what the flake had been hiding. The pattern of a fern stood out clearly where the piece had fallen away.

She touched it. The shape felt as if it had been carved, but Nim knew that wasn't true. This fern had been a living leaf once upon a time, until it had been covered with mud, and slowly, over thousands and millions of years, it had turned into a fossil.

Her fingers tingled, knowing she was touching something that had lived so long ago. It wasn't very big, but maybe there was another one beside it – maybe even a bigger one. She could bring Edmund back up here to help her search. He couldn't always keep quiet enough to find live animals, but he couldn't scare off a dead plant.

And when they showed everyone else… She imagined Leonora saying, 'I've never seen such a perfect fossil! That's exactly the clue we need to find a biofuel.'

A hand's breadth away from the fern there was a bulge in the rock. Nim ran her fingers over it. She could feel an edge, and the more she rubbed, the more she could feel.

'It's a branch,' she told Fred. 'It must be a giant fern. I wonder if I'm the first person who ever found a giant fern fossil?'

Fred didn't answer, even with a sneeze. The cave was cold, and Fred was cold blooded: it was getting hard for him to move.

'Sorry, Fred,' said Nim. 'Time for you to soak up some sunshine.' She rubbed the edge of the bulge one last time, and a drift of soft limestone crumbled away. The branch was even bigger than she'd thought.

Nim forgot that Fred was cold and Selkie was worried. She rubbed around the edge. She spat the dirt off her hands and rubbed again.

More rock crumbled away. The bulge bulged bigger. It was more like a log than a branch.

Selkie barked again. *If you don't come out now, I'll come in!* that bark said.

Nim left her fossil and raced back around the stalagmite. Finding her way out would be easy, because a bit of daylight should be coming down the tunnel from the entrance.

There was no daylight; no way out.

I'm trapped! Nim thought – just for a second, but it was a long second. And then she realised: there was no daylight because the door hole was completely blocked by a sea lion's head and shoulders.

'Go back, Selkie!' Nim shouted. If Selkie got stuck, they'd all be here forever, until they turned into fossils too.

Selkie humphed, backed up – and finally there was light. Nim slid through the hole and lay on the path, blinking in the bright sunshine. The sea lion sniffed and checked her. Fred gave a pathetic snort of sneeze.

But they had no time to waste. Bright sunshine meant it was time to get back to the house, and then to the camp.

Chapter 6

EDMUND HAD BEEN telling the truth when he said that he liked being alone.

But he loved camping alone even more than he'd imagined. He loved having his own tiny tent, with nothing in it except his pack, sleeping bag, and four interesting shells he'd picked up on the beach yesterday. He kept the tent flap open all night so he could see the stars, and hear the sea whispering through his dreams.

It would have been perfect if Tiffany and Tristan hadn't been around. He'd only been on the island for two days the first time he came, and for most of it Nim hadn't liked him at all. He didn't quite know how to be friends with her in front of other kids.

The other not-quite-perfect part was thinking about Dr Ashburn and Professor Hunterstone. He'd only met them once, but he liked them. Now he kept thinking of Selina's voice on the phone yesterday. 'It's okay,' she'd said, even though she'd already had to stop talking once to run and be sick. 'Lance and Leonora can do the science just as well as Peter and I can. And they'll take you with them to meet the Lowes and their boat – they're very kind.'

The problem was that Edmund couldn't like Leonora and Lance. He didn't exactly *not* like them, but his skin prickled whenever they were around. It was uncomfortable having prickly skin.

HE SLIPPED BETWEEN the tents and down to the beach. The sun was rising pink and gold behind Fire Mountain, but in front of him the sky was a pale grey-blue, and so was the sea. The tide was washing the beach fresh and clean. Edmund felt the sand tickle between his toes. Only a bird had been there before him; when he turned around his footprints were beside the pattern of its webbed feet, as if he'd been walking with his pet seagull.

It would be good to have a bird as a friend, he thought, like Nim had Fred and Selkie. Edmund had a dog at home, a goofy, loving labrador named Sam, who was as much a part of the family as anyone else. But there was

something wild and wonderful about Nim's animal friends. They were free to do whatever they wanted, and what they wanted was to be with Nim.

At the end of the beach was a point of worn grey rocks covered with sea lions. Some of them were sliding into the water for their morning fish, some were dozing and some were watching him – but they were all big, and there were a lot of them.

'I'm a friend of Nim's,' Edmund told them. 'And Selkie's.'

It was hard to tell if the sea lions had understood. Edmund decided to walk on the grass for a while.

On the other side of the point, the reef met the rocks in a huge ring. The sea shushed in and out through a hole in the reef, but inside the cove, the water was so calm and clear that he could see the sand and giant clams on the bottom, and the sea horses and tiny bright fish darting in between.

Edmund stood on the edge of the rocks watching them. He lay on his stomach and went on watching. Finally he jumped in. He swam with the polka-dot fish and dived down to see the clams up close. He floated on his back and let the sun warm him, and swam and dived again. He had never felt so free.

NIM MET JACK and Alex on the trail home.

'I wanted to walk now if I'm going to hide in my studio all day,' Alex explained.

Nim hated the thought of being stuck anywhere that long, even somewhere like Alex's studio, with its big open windows looking out to the forest.

'I guess I'd rather meet people than stay inside,' she said.

'Even Tiff-Tris?' Jack teased.

Nim didn't think there was anything funny about the twins.

'I guess so,' she said. 'At least their little brother is cute. He's a lot nicer than they are.'

'Everyone has something good in them,' said Alex. 'Some people just hide it at first.'

'Luckily you've got two days to find it,' said Jack. 'Because I want you to stay with the other kids and make sure they don't fall into any trouble while they're here.'

Nim knew there was no point in arguing – but at least they'd forgotten to ask where she'd been. She decided to wait and tell them about the fern fossil later. A surprise like that would be a present for Jack as much as for Leonora. Even more, because it would always be here on the island.

In fact, it was such a good present that Nim decided she didn't feel guilty about going somewhere dangerous without telling anyone.

THE OTHER TWO tents were still closed and quiet when Edmund got back to the camp. He took his water bottle and toothbrush up to the freshwater pool. He filled the bottle at the waterfall and brushed his teeth out on the hill. Looking down over the grasslands to the sea was much better than looking at the bathroom sink at home.

But he'd already used half his water. He went back to the waterfall. Nim was there filling a bottle too.

'Did you fall in?' she asked.

Edmund had forgotten he was still wet. 'I went swimming in Keyhole Cove – it was amazing! I saw sea horses, and clown fish, and ...' His voice trickled away when he saw Nim's expression. 'Was that okay?'

Nim didn't know how to say that she'd been imagining how much he'd like it when she showed it to him, and now he'd spoiled it by finding it himself. 'Just don't take Tiffany and Tristan,' she said.

'They're too cool to go anywhere with me anyway.'

'But Jack said all the scientists are going to do science stuff all day,' Nim began.

'And the kids are supposed to hang together?' asked Edmund.

Nim pictured them all hanging upside down like the bats in the cave. She laughed, but it didn't change the problem. It was her job to keep the other kids safe on her island, but if Tiffany and Tristan mocked one more thing she truly might explode – she didn't want to share her discovery with them until she knew exactly what it was and how good it was.

But if she didn't share it now, she wouldn't have time to figure out exactly what she'd found before everyone left.

She wanted to show her fossil to Leonora more than she didn't want to spend the day with the twins.

And maybe, just maybe, they'd be different after spending a night on the island. Maybe they'd wake up realising what a special place it was, and how amazing Selkie and Fred were. Maybe they'd even want to be friends.

'It'll be okay,' Nim told him. 'I've got something really cool to show you. Even Tiff-Tris will think so.'

BACK AT THE camp, everyone was busy getting up and deciding what they should do for the day.

Anika wanted to take their boat out to study the algae on the faraway reef and compare it to those living on the coral around the island. Ryan wanted to test water samples and temperatures all the way in between.

'I'll take you,' said Jack. 'The sailboat won't disturb the water the way a motorboat does.'

'No more boat!' said Ollie.

'You can stay with Tiff-Tris,' said their mother.

'But…' the twins whined.

'We'll be working,' Anika told them. 'Ollie will be much safer here with you than on the boat. Take him to the beach, or whatever you want – just keep an eye on him.'

'I've got two eyes!' said Ollie, holding up two fingers.

'So do I,' Nim said. She smiled and held up two fingers too.

'And I'm this much old,' said Ollie, putting up three fingers.

Human babies take a lot longer to grow up than sea lions and iguanas! Nim thought.

Jack grinned at her as if he knew what she was thinking.

'Where do you want to explore?' he asked Lance and Leonora.

'The cliffs and the mountain,' said Lance. 'Whether it's algae in rock pools or some other undiscovered vegetation, the perfect source of biofuel must be out there somewhere.'

'Unless you have any ideas for us, Nim?' asked Leonora.

Nim shook her head. It would completely spoil the surprise if they came with her.

But she wasn't used to keeping secrets, and she knew her face was glowing as hot and red as a frigate bird's throat. She hid it against Selkie's warm neck.

Hmphh! Selkie snorted. She knew that Nim wasn't really cuddling her.

When Anika and Ryan had sailed off with Jack, and Lance and Leonora were in their tent getting ready for the day, Nim announced to the others that she had something amazing to show them.

'What kind of amazing?' asked Tiffany.

Tiffany's voice was quite loud. Nim beckoned for them all to come further away from the tents.

'A cave,' she whispered.

'Cool!' Tristan started to say, but stopped when his sister glared at him.

'We'll have to be quiet because of the bats,' Nim added.

'Bats!' Tiffany shrieked.

'Just the mothers and babies,' Nim explained. 'They're sleeping now it's day, so we can't disturb them.'

'So why would we want to go there?' Tiffany demanded.

'I think I've found a fossil,' said Nim.

'And you want us to help dig it out?' Tristan asked.

'We can't dig out the walls in a bat nursery!' Nim shouted, horrified. She remembered that she was trying to be quiet and started again. 'I want to clean it up so we can see it.'

'If you show it to Leonora, she'll want to take it out,' Tiffany said.

'No, she won't,' Nim snapped. She didn't understand why Tiffany had to be so nasty about Leonora. 'Jack said everyone had agreed: the research is just observation. No one can do anything that changes the island.'

Edmund nodded. 'That's what Dr Ashburn said.'

'And we got about sixteen hundred lectures about it before we came,' said Tristan. 'So let's go see the cave.'

Nim breathed a sigh of relief. She hadn't meant to snap, because she really needed them to go with her. *Stay with them and make sure they're safe*, Jack had said.

'But we're supposed to be looking after Ollie,' said Tiffany. 'I'm not taking him all the way back up the mountain.'

Ollie had dug a big hole in the sand. Now he was sitting in it and using a plastic mug to pour the sand back in from the edges. Nim trickled a handful over his toes as she tried to stop the volcano inside her from exploding.

They're only here for two more days. That was the other thing Jack had said. *Even Fire Mountain can last that long without erupting.*

Fire Mountain hasn't met Tiffany, Nim thought rebelliously.

So FIFTEEN MINUTES later, when Tiffany was still telling Tristan they couldn't go and Tristan was saying he could piggyback Ollie, and Tiffany was saying all over again that she wasn't going into a cave with bats for anything, and it probably wasn't a real fossil anyway, a bit of steam hissed out of Nim's eyes, and she said she didn't care what anyone else did, she was going.

'So am I,' said Edmund, coming out of his tent with his daypack.

'We're not,' said Tiffany.

Tristan looked miserable and didn't say anything.

Ollie was too busy burying his legs in the sand to listen.

NIM WAITED A few more minutes, until Leonora and Lance had come out of their tent and waved goodbye. They were heading towards Frigate Bird Cliffs. *Perfect!* Nim thought. She and Edmund were going exactly the opposite direction. And she'd asked the others to come – it wasn't her fault they were staying behind.

She was nearly singing as she picked up her backpack. It had her bamboo drinker full of fresh water, two bananas, a big chunk of coconut and a chisel from her toolbox.

'Would Fred ride on my shoulder?' Edmund asked.

'He might if you give him this,' Nim said, breaking off a piece of coconut.

Edmund sat down beside the iguana and held out the coconut. Fred grabbed it and gulped it down. He looked across at Nim.

'It's okay,' she said. 'You can go with Edmund for a while.'

Fred scampered up to Edmund's shoulder. Edmund stood up carefully, and felt the small sharp nails clinging. 'You're tickling!'

Nim laughed. She was so used to Fred that she hardly felt the tickle anymore, but she'd never thought how it would feel to someone else. It was almost as if she'd never seen him properly before. A bubble of love swelled inside her for her small spiky friend.

Her big smooth friend wasn't nearly so happy. Selkie humphed and snorted when Nim told her they were going back to the caves. 'You could stay with Tiff-Tris and Ollie,' Nim said.

The sea lion snorted even harder and galumphed down to the sea without looking back.

Chapter 7

ALEX STARED OUT of her studio window. The rainforest
was cool and green, but Alex was writing. All she saw
was the hot dry desert that her Hero and his camel were
trudging across, tired and thirsty...

'That's ridiculous!' she scolded herself. 'They'll never
get there in time.'

If her Hero didn't find the treasure and stop the Bad
Guys from blowing up the temple, that would be the end
of the story, and it wasn't the end Alex wanted.

Now the Hero was riding and the camel was galloping.
Puffs of sand flew up from the camel's hooves; the air was
hot in the Hero's face.

'That's better,' said Alex. She watched him gallop
through the narrow streets of the ancient city and leap off
at the temple door.

'But now the camel will die if the dynamite goes off!'

Worse, the temple and the square around it were
crowded with people. The Bad Guys didn't care – they just
wanted to blow it up to get the treasure they thought was
buried beneath it.

Her Hero had to be smart as well as brave. He had to make sure that everyone else was safe before he risked his own life to save a building.

He turned the camel around and whacked it on the rump. 'Shoo!' he shouted, waving his arms till the camel ran and everyone raced out to follow it to safety.

The Bad Guys were fleeing out the back of the temple. They'd set the dynamite just before the Hero got there.

He's not going to be searching for treasure when the building's about to blow up, Alex thought. *But if he saves the temple, maybe he somehow uses the dynamite to catch*

the Bad Guys – and that's when he realises he's found the treasure. Right now he doesn't have time for anything except finding the dynamite and making a lightning decision about what to do.

Which was why she had to work out how much time he needed.

If the temple is ten times as big as my studio, then the treasure would be hidden under that tree near the path ... I'll time how long it takes Nim to run from the tree to the door. Running through the forest will be like running around all the statues and things in the temple.

But they couldn't do the test today because of the visitors. That reminded her, there was something she was going to look up, something to do with Nim and whatever she'd been doing this morning. Because as soon as she'd seen her coming back down the trail so early, Alex knew Nim was up to something. She just didn't know what.

She shook her head. She still couldn't remember what she'd meant to look up – it mustn't have been important.

Alex turned over the page, and started sketching a plan of the temple.

EDMUND WAS TELLING Nim about his school. Nim had read lots of books about schools, but it was different when Edmund told it. She'd never really imagined what it would be like to sit at a desk for a whole hour. 'But don't you ever feel like you're going to burst if you don't get up and run around?'

Edmund laughed. 'All the time,' he said, so even though she wasn't quite sure why he was laughing, she knew that he wasn't laughing at her. It was a whole lot easier being friends when they were alone.

'Wait for me!'

Tristan was jogging across the grasslands behind them. They stopped for him to catch up.

'Are Tiffany and Ollie coming too?' asked Nim.

Tristan shook his head. 'I don't have to do everything Tiff says.'

Nim led them through the rainforest, wide around the Hissing Stones, where the yellow pool splattered its slimy bubbles and steamy water fountained high. They couldn't go wide enough to miss the stink. It smelled as if a hundred rotten eggs had all smashed at once.

Tristan held his nose. Edmund looked as if he wanted to. Fred sneezed. They were all glad to get to the Black Rocks.

The boys weren't as used to rock climbing as Nim; Edmund slipped off one rock and skidded down another before he got his balance.

'Sorry, Fred,' he said, patting the spiny head.

Fred rubbed against his neck. Fred liked sliding.

At the top of the cliff they stopped. They could see far over the sea, and over the rocks they'd just climbed, and south to the rainforest that Nim had climbed that morning.

Below was the deep sea, where Nim and Fred had dived to save Selkie from the Troppo Tourists. Further along, the sharp rocks formed a small cove, but it was not a calm and peaceful place like Keyhole Cove. This was the island's wild side, and it could never quite be trusted.

They climbed on up the path to the door hole of Nim's new cave.

'I thought you said it was big!' said Edmund.

'Just wait till you get inside,' said Nim.

She put on her headlamp and slid in through the hole. She slid a bit faster than she meant to, because of showing the boys how, and landed harder than her knees wanted. She spat on her hands and rubbed the blood off before anyone saw.

Tristan followed, pulling a mini torch out of his pocket. Edmund put on a headlamp and slid through last, with Fred still on his shoulder.

Nim stopped in the glowing cavern for them to catch up. Tristan was staring around in awe: he bumped into her, then Edmund bumped into him, and then Fred got frightened and jumped from Edmund's shoulder to Tristan's and across to Nim.

'Ouch!' said Tristan. Fred's claws weren't actually sharper when he was frightened, but he dug them in deeper.

'Don't disturb the bats!' Nim shushed, rubbing Fred's head.

She slipped around the big stalagmite into the side tunnel. Her headlamp lit up the leaf pattern in the rock.

Edmund shrugged his daypack off his back and pulled out a paintbrush.

'You can't paint it!' Nim hissed.

'I can do something better,' said Edmund.

Very gently, he began brushing the wall around the fossil. Whitish dust drifted away, and the pattern stood out as clearly as if it had just been pressed into clay. It wasn't a fern – it was seaweed.

'Cool!' said Tristan. 'What's that other thing?'

On the wall where Edmund had started brushing, a spark of blue danced in the torchlight.

'Oh,' Nim said sadly. She ran her fingers over the bulge that she'd thought might be a fossilised branch. But she was very sure that fossils weren't blue, and just as sure that something this big couldn't be anything to do with the delicate sea plant.

Tristan rubbed with his hand, and Edmund started brushing again. More blue appeared, with sparks of fire dancing inside it.

'It's an opal!' Edmund exclaimed.

They all ran their hands over the wall, feeling from the ridge where the blue started, up, down and along.

'It's huge!' Tristan breathed.

Nim was still disappointed that it wasn't a fossil, but the more of the fiery blue she saw, the more beautiful it seemed. She got out her chisel and chipped gently away at the rock above where whatever-it-was began.

Edmund got a smaller brush out of his daypack and gave it to Tristan.

'I've got a comb too,' said Tristan, and they all laughed. But even as they joked about brushing and combing the rock's hair, they kept on doing it. The shape stood out more and more clearly as the boys brushed away the flakes of rock that fell from Nim's chisel. Then Tristan ran his comb over the bulge itself, and when Edmund brushed those dirt crumbs away, more sparks of blue and green glowed from the wall.

They went on working. When Nim had chiselled all around the outside of the shape, she used the spike on her pocketknife to pry the last bits of limestone away from the edges. The boys went on brushing. The opal grew and grew.

'It's like finding buried treasure!' Tristan exclaimed.

After a while they stopped to eat the coconut and bananas, and an energy bar Tristan had in his pocket. Then they went on uncovering whatever was on the wall.

It was a round shape, longer than Nim could spread her arms wide, and curved out gently in the middle.

'Here's something else,' said Edmund, brushing just below it.

Very delicately, Nim picked around it with her spike. Edmund flicked the crumbs off, brushing and brushing until a long, thin piece of opal appeared.

'It looks like a bone,' said Tristan.

Edmund brushed a bit more. The blue-green, sparking-with-red opal was long and thin and knobbly.

'Like a tailbone,' said Nim.

Edmund brushed more carefully still, flicking out the grains of dirt around the knobbles.

Nim went back to the big shape. She'd uncovered the outside nearly all the way around now: an oval ring of hard, shining stone in the softer rock of the wall. There was a wide band across the middle, and ribs of colour stretching across from the band to the outer edge. She ran her hands over the whole thing again.

It was the same shape as Chica's shell.

Nim stood back and let the light of her headlamp rove slowly over the wall. 'It's a sea turtle,' she said at last.

'Fossilised into opal,' Edmund said slowly, still brushing.

'And not just the shell,' said Tristan. 'I've found its head.'

They all stood back and stared. The shape Tristan was uncovering was oblong ... exactly like a skull. At the other end of the shell, Edmund had just brushed away the dirt from a longer bone, with a ray of smaller bones sprouting from the end.

'Sea turtles don't have fingers, do they?' Edmund asked.

'No,' said Nim. 'But Jack says the bones inside their flippers are pretty much the same as our feet and toes.'

They all stared at it for a long time. 'Wow,' Tristan said at last. 'That's the coolest thing I've ever seen.'

'I was hoping it was going to be a fern tree branch,' Nim admitted.

'That's too bad,' said Edmund, sounding so serious that for a moment Nim was tricked. 'You wanted a bit of fern and instead you got a whole opal fossil sea turtle. Probably the rarest fossil in the whole world.'

Tristan laughed, and that made Edmund start and then Nim. Even when they got out their water bottles they kept spluttering and leaking water out of their mouths while they drank.

Finally Edmund pulled out his camera and started taking pictures. Tristan and Nim shone the lights on the fossil so the glowing opal flashed sparks of fire against the darkness.

'Chica's great-great – millions of great – grandmother,' Nim said softly. 'Now she's like a secret jewel inside the mountain.'

'She *is* a jewel,' said Edmund.

LEONORA AND LANCE had headed off towards Frigate Bird Cliffs, just like they said. But they hadn't said how far they were going, and they didn't go very far at all. At the first hollow, they sat down to wait. Every few minutes one of them would lie on their stomach and peek over the rise to spy on the camp with Lance's binoculars.

Because Leonora had been studying Nim ever since they arrived on the island, and she was sure that Nim was hiding something. Especially this morning when she'd heard bits of whispered words: *fossil … amazing … cave.*

So what they wanted to explore was whatever Nim didn't want them to see.

They watched Selkie go down to the ocean and Nim and Edmund head across the grasslands.

'The twins have stayed behind!' Lance said in disgust. 'That's going to complicate things.'

'They're just kids,' said Leonora. 'We won't have any trouble outsmarting them.'

They thought for a few minutes. 'If it's part of the cave we went to yesterday, we can go up the hill and around so the twins don't see us.'

'But we'll be able to catch up so we can see exactly where Nim is going.'

Lance poked his binoculars over the lip of the hollow again. The camp appeared empty, but he glimpsed the back of a dark head as Tristan disappeared around a grassy hill.

'Even better!' he laughed. 'One thing's for sure, those twins stick together. If you see one, you know the other's there too.'

'And with five kids to follow, it's going to be that much easier to spot one of them ...'

'... and let them lead us to whatever it is they've found.'

They smiled smugly as they climbed out of their hollow. They couldn't see the group but it didn't matter now they'd guessed where they were heading. Once, when they pulled out their binoculars, they saw Nim starting to climb the Black Rocks. They waited out of sight in the rainforest until they guessed everyone was at the top.

By the time they'd climbed the rocks too, they were just in time to see Edmund's legs sliding into a hole in the side of the cliff. 'That was lucky!' said Lance. 'I told you,' said Leonora. 'I've got a very good feeling about this.' They waited a few more minutes, and then crept carefully up the path to the cave. For a long, long time, they sat outside, taking turns to stick their heads through the door hole and listen.

Chapter 8

TIFFANY WAS BORED. She'd taken Ollie down to the water, and they'd waded and splashed. It was hot enough to swim, but Ollie couldn't swim and Tiff couldn't leave him alone while she swam. She didn't find wading and splashing nearly as exciting as the three-year-old did.

When Ollie was tired they went back to the tent; Tiffany tucked her little brother into his sleeping sheet, and lay down on hers. There was nothing else to do. All the batteries were flat; she couldn't listen to music, couldn't send messages, couldn't read.

Maybe she should have gone with Tris and the others, she thought. But she didn't like caves, and she really was afraid of bats. She kept imagining them dropping off the ceiling in the darkness, landing on her head, tangling in her hair. She shuddered just thinking about it.

Finally she found a book her mum had been reading. It was about the life span of coral, and it was mostly charts and graphs. It was better than thinking about bats, but there were so many Latin words and the sentences were so long that Tiffany had to close her eyes between each paragraph. After a while it was too much trouble to open them again. Tiffany dropped the book and slept.

Through a dream, she heard voices, and the rustle of a tent flap.

'It was lucky I spotted that bratty twin going with them,' Lance was saying. 'They might have got suspicious if they'd seen us heading off again with all our gear.'

Suddenly Tiffany was wide awake. She lay still as stone, hardly breathing. Her ears stretched and strained to catch every word.

'We'd have just had to deal with them here,' said Leonora. 'If the kids are right about what they've got in that cave, this could be the find of the century!'

'We'll do whatever it takes to make sure it's yours,' Lance agreed. 'And if we can't get the fossil out whole, we'll have a big pile of opal to sell.'

'As long as they know what they're talking about ... we should have gone all the way into the tunnel and seen it for ourselves. I'll be very annoyed if we haul these tools all the way up there for nothing.'

'It's better this way. Kids get bored easily – they're probably gone by now. If not, it'll be much easier to deal with them when we've got our ropes.'

Tiffany's body was still frozen, but her mind was racing. *Deal with them? With ropes?* She was suddenly very afraid. She didn't care what Nim had found in that bat cave, she didn't care what fossils or opals Leonora wanted, but she cared, more than she'd ever known she could, when someone threatened her brother.

Now she was even angrier than she was afraid.

As silently as she could, she got up from her mat. She put on her sneakers, shoved her mini torch into her pocket, her sunhat onto her head, and a water bottle into a pouch on her belt. Ollie was still sound asleep in his sheet. Tiffany slid her arms under it and very gently picked up her little brother.

'What are we doing?' Ollie murmured, without opening his eyes.

'Shh,' Tiffany whispered. 'We're playing a game. You're the baby koala and I'm the mummy. You have to be sound asleep riding on my back.'

The noises from the other tent sounded as if Lance and Leonora were packing. There were thumps and rustles, and mutters of, 'We'll have to get away fast if we use it, but it'll be worth it,' and, 'We'll need the net to lower it off the cliff'.

Tiffany wiggled Ollie in his sheet around to her back. She knotted the bottom of the sheet around her waist, and the top around her shoulders. Even with the sling, Ollie was heavy.

'Hang on, Baby Koala,' she whispered.

She tiptoed to the tent door. Her heart was beating so loudly she was afraid that Lance and Leonora would hear it. *Just stay here and hide*, whispered a voice in her head. *You'll be safe here – and Tris will probably be all right.*

But he might not be. That was the truth. If she didn't warn him about the Bijous, her twin could be in terrible danger. She put her hand on the tent flap. The Bijous' tent was facing away from hers, but that meant she couldn't peek into it and run when they were facing the other way. Sticking her head out was going to be the most terrifying thing she'd ever done.

'I can't believe how easy they're making this for us!' Leonora laughed. 'Anika and Ryan are just as sweet and stupid as Selina and Peter – and Jack's so simple he's left all his research in that cave. It's as if he *wants* someone to destroy it!'

'I'm happy to help out,' Lance said grimly. 'I've been a fuel engineer all my life and I'm not going to have algae ruin my plans!'

'Opal fossils for me, no competition for you,' Leonora gloated. 'Coming here is working out even better than we'd hoped!'

There were no more choices.

Tiffany crouched, bounded out of the tent and started running. She raced right across the grasslands without stopping, her little brother bouncing on her back. By the time she reached the safety of the first trees she was gasping for breath. Ollie rolled out of the sling as she sank to her knees in the soft forest litter. He looked around, and squeezed his eyes tight shut again.

'You can wake up now,' Tiffany panted, looking anxiously over her shoulder for any sign of the Bijous. 'We'll play a different game.'

'Aren't I a baby koala anymore?'

'Now you're...' Tiffany tried to think of the quietest, fastest animal she could. She didn't want to start hopping like a rabbit or slithering like a snake. 'We're quiet little mice, and we're going to go through the forest as fast as we can without anyone hearing us.'

'Why?' asked Ollie.

'Because there's a great big cat that wants to eat us up,' said Tiffany. *But it would be a lot easier if the mice knew where they were going!*

She didn't say that part out loud.

This morning she'd thought Nim was talking about a new cave, but Leonora and Lance seemed to be talking about the Emergency Cave. The problem was that Tiffany hadn't paid much attention when they were there yesterday. She knew the cave was on top of the Black Rocks, but she couldn't exactly remember how they'd got back from there.

All she knew for sure was that Tristan had disappeared in this direction. There was a bit of trail going up the hill. *Please let it be the right one!* Tiff thought to herself.

Ollie was crawling up it already. 'This is how mice run!'

'These mice run faster on their legs,' said Tiffany.

The little boy obediently raced past her, running as hard as he could. Sticks snapped and branches twanged. A tree root caught his foot – but Tiffany leapt and scooped him up before he hit the ground.

'That was fast like a horse!' she whispered.

Ollie wrapped his arms around her neck and rested his face against hers. 'You're my nice horse sister,' he said.

He sounded so surprised that Tiffany flushed. She staggered on carrying him, until her right foot stepped in a hole and her left foot skidded, and she sat down hard. Her bottom hurt and somehow she'd thumped her funny bone, which wasn't funny at all. But at least she hadn't twisted an ankle. She bit her lip and got back up.

'Ready to walk quietly as a mouse?' she whispered. 'Look – this is my tail.' She unknotted the top of the sling so that the sheet flowed out like a cape from her waist.

'Where's my tail?' Ollie whined.

'I'll get you a good one later. Promise. But now the baby mouse holds onto the sister mouse's tail.'

'So it's my tail too,' Ollie said.

'Okay,' said Tiffany. 'Just hold onto it. And remember the game – we don't want the cat to hear us. So we can't step on sticks, or fall down, or talk more.'

She started off again, walking fast. Ollie held the sheet and jogged behind her. The trail climbed steeply. They'd stopped and started so often that Tiffany had no idea how long they'd been walking, or if they were still going the right direction.

I don't even know how I'm going to know! she thought despairingly. Whichever way she looked, the forest was the same: just trees and vines and ferns ... and the bowerbird's nest. The pile of sticks decorated with yellow flowers and berries, where Nim had glared at her just because she'd taken one little flower.

But today it was the bowerbird who'd stolen something new. Placed carefully in front of the bower was a scorpion, trapped forever in a big amber necklace.

Leonora and Lance went by here this morning!
We're going the right way.

Ollie darted ahead and grabbed the pendant. The bird stared fiercely from beside his bower.

'Put it back!' Tiffany hissed. 'It's not yours.'

'You took the flower,' Ollie reminded her.

'That's different!'

But Tiffany didn't want to touch the necklace, and Ollie wouldn't let it go.

'It's my mouse tail,' he said, slipping the chain over his head with the scorpion at the back. It bounced along behind his bottom, just the right place for a tail.

For half a second, Tiffany forgot how afraid she was, and laughed. It felt good. She took her brother's hand, and they hurried on.

A few minutes later, they smelled the rotten-egg stink of the Hissing Stones and saw the start of the Black Rocks.

Reaching the Black Rocks was good because it meant they were getting close to the cave, but bad because there was nowhere to hide. Once she and Ollie started to climb, the Bijous would be able to see them from nearly anywhere on this side of the island.

Tiffany stopped under the last tree of the rainforest and listened. There were bird sounds, ocean sounds and Hissing Stones sounds. There were no people sounds – but Lance and Leonora were smart enough to be quiet if they were following her. *What if they're right behind us and I just can't hear them?*

But she couldn't turn around now, and she couldn't let Ollie see how afraid she was.

'Now,' she whispered, 'we're going to be monkeys and climb up those rocks before a big gorilla catches us!'

TIFFANY WASN'T STRONG enough to climb the Black Rocks with Ollie on her back. They each needed both hands to climb, so they couldn't hold hands and he couldn't hold onto the end of the sheet. But Ollie was so little and the rocks were so big, that she was afraid to let him go by himself.

She unknotted the sleeping bag sheet from around her waist, and ripped the sides open into one long skinny strip. She knotted one end around Ollie's middle and the other around hers.

They began to climb.

The boulders were round and rough, piled like stacks of marbles; sometimes Tiffany needed her hands to balance and sometimes she could scramble up without them. Sometimes she stopped and pulled Ollie right up beside her before she started again.

'I like climbing rocks!' said Ollie.

'So do I,' said Tiffany. It would have been true if she hadn't been so terrified of who might be climbing behind them.

But she couldn't stop and look till they reached the top. It seemed to take forever – and when she was finally standing on the cliff path, the breeze was blowing the trees too hard to see into the rainforest, and the surf was thundering too hard to hear. She still couldn't know for sure that Lance and Leonora weren't close behind.

But ahead, leading into the hillside, was the mouth of a cave.

Tiffany breathed a sigh of relief. 'Tris is going to be so surprised to see us!' she said, and they walked into the darkness.

There was no one there. Tiffany turned on her torch, and shone it all around. It lit up dark stone walls, a hard stone floor, shelves of test tubes and neat stacks of canned food. They walked right around it, touching the walls, just to make sure – but there were no secret passageways or tunnels. There weren't even any bats.

This was the Emergency Cave she'd waited outside yesterday. The bats and the fossil were in a completely different cave.

'Where's Tris?' Ollie demanded.

'I don't know,' said Tiff.

It was the saddest thing she'd ever said. She'd raced through the forest and climbed all the way up here with her little brother, and it was the wrong place.

'Are we going to look for him?' asked Ollie.

'Yes,' said Tiffany. 'He can't be far away.'

But Nim had lived on the island her whole life and she'd only found the fossil cave yesterday. Now Tiffany had to find it before the Bijous did. She stood at the cave entrance, her heart thumping.

The path above her was narrower; rainforest trees leaned over it and even dangled over the cliff. When they'd come down that way yesterday, she hadn't seen anything that could possibly be the opening to a cave.

Maybe they'd already passed it.

She had to decide.

She leaned out over the cliff. Lance and Leonora were still nowhere in sight.

Holding Ollie tightly by the hand, Tiffany inched her way back down the way they had come. They looked into cracks that lizards couldn't have slithered through. They poked into holes full of leaves and grit. They stared at the walls of the cliff and the mounds of boulders until their eyes watered. They went back up the path to where the trees began.

Now even the weather seemed to know her search was hopeless. The bright blue sky had turned dark; the sun was covered with threatening clouds.

Finally Tiffany went back to the Emergency Cave. There were still no mysterious tunnels; no hidden entrances to other caves. And no Tristan.

Tiffany hugged Ollie close as she slid down onto the cold stone floor. She couldn't stop Lance and Leonora from stealing whatever they wanted to steal and hurting whoever got in their way. Her twin was in danger – and now she'd put her little brother in danger too. She tried not to cry, but once she started she couldn't stop, no matter how much Ollie patted her face.

After a while Ollie started crying too.

SELKIE WAS IN the rocky cove below the Black Rocks. It wasn't her favourite place for fishing, but she wasn't there for fish. She was patrolling, watching the entrance to the cave and listening for Nim's whistle.

A boat was coming. It was the boat that had come to the island yesterday – Nim and Jack had let it land, so Selkie knew that she had to leave it alone. But she didn't like it. She didn't like boats with motors, and she didn't like that it was coming into this cove when Nim didn't know. She dived as it anchored and poked her head up again just enough to watch Leonora and Lance unload the ropes and gear into the rubber dinghy.

They paddled in to shore and pulled the dinghy up onto the rocks. 'If those brats have truly found something worthwhile, we'll lower it down to here, and take off,' said Lance.

'But before we go,' said Leonora, 'it'll be goodbye to Jack's laboratory and all those algae!'

Lance strapped the pack onto his back, and they started up the cliff.

Chapter 9

NIM, EDMUND AND Tristan were still brushing and polishing the sea turtle fossil so the opal gleamed brighter and its fires leapt further. Fred was scrambling from one person's shoulder to another, trying to catch glow-worms.

Suddenly Tristan froze. 'I can hear something.'

They all stopped and listened. They could hear their own breathing; nothing else.

'I'm going out to see,' said Tristan.

'I'm going on working,' said Nim, and Edmund agreed. The turtle was so beautiful that they wanted it to be perfect, and every time they brushed one bit, another bit that needed brushing showed through.

Tristan crouched through the tunnel and crawled out the door hole. The sunshine was blinding after the hours of darkness; he leaned against the side of the hill as he waited for his eyes to work again, and listened.

He'd told Nim and Edmund that he'd heard something because he didn't know how else to explain the feeling. It was like a warning siren inside him: *Something's wrong! Pay attention.* But outside, he could almost hear it with his ears. It was a very faint, gasping noise, like the sound that Ollie made when he'd cried so much he couldn't cry any more.

The only other time Tristan had ever felt anything like this was when he and Tiff were seven. He'd been at a friend's house when Tiff had fallen off the monkey bars and broken her arm. Tris hadn't waited to tell his friend he was leaving: he'd just run all the way to the playground. He'd got there just as his mum's car disappeared around the corner on the way to the hospital.

He'd never forgotten that feeling.

So he headed down the hill now, still listening. Whatever it was sounded more and more like sobbing, and by the time he got to the Emergency Cave, Tristan was running so fast he skidded right past the entrance.

'Tris?'

He spun around. His sister and brother were huddled on the floor.

'How come you weren't here before?' Ollie demanded. 'We were going to give you a big surprise!'

'You did,' said Tristan.

Tiffany sniffed, wiped her nose on the back of her arm, and stood up. 'Something terrible's happened. Lance and Leonora want whatever it is you've found, and they say nothing's going to stop them.'

TRISTAN LED THE way back up the path, faster than they'd ever thought they could walk at the top of a cliff.

He turned where two sticks lay crossed in front of a tree, and disappeared through the hole in the rock.

'I thought I'd looked everywhere,' Tiffany said bitterly. 'But I went right past it!' She boosted Ollie in through the hole, and slid in after him.

There was a boom of thunder. The first fat raindrops chased her through the hole into suffocating darkness. If she hadn't been tied to her little brother Tiff would have climbed right back out again. She'd rather be wet than cramped in a low, dank tunnel.

Tristan turned on his torch. 'The fossil is on the other side of the wall, right about here.'

'But we've got to go down the tunnel to get there?' Tiffany asked, pulling her own torch out of her pocket.

Before she'd had time to switch it on, Tris and his light turned into the side tunnel. Ollie followed close to his brother, and for a second, as Tiff stepped into the vast, eerily glimmering cavern, she was alone. She forgot the bats, she forgot Lance and Leonora, she forgot to be afraid. She felt as if she'd stepped into an enchanted world, and she didn't know yet if it was good or evil.

Then the sheet around her waist tugged her along, and she hurried around the bend.

Nim and Edmund stepped back in surprise as Tristan appeared with Ollie. Their lights shone on the huge opal turtle, and when Tristan added his, the blues and greens gleamed as if the sea was caught in the rock, with hints of fire flashing from the heart of Fire Mountain itself.

Nim prickled. She didn't want Tiffany here. This was the most special thing she'd ever discovered. Every time she rubbed another little bit clear – another vertebra in the turtle's neck, or a deeper patch of colour on the shell, excitement bubbled up in her all over again. Now Tiffany was going to say something sarcastic and wreck that feeling.

'Wow,' Tiffany breathed, exactly like Tristan had. 'That's the coolest thing I've ever seen.'

Nim waited. 'Really?' she asked at last.

'Totally,' said Tiffany. She touched the turtle's shell with a careful finger, as if she were stroking a butterfly – and the coldness of the touch seemed to wake her up.

'This is terrible!' she said urgently.

Nim bristled again.

'It's so amazing, the Bijous are going to want it for sure. They're coming to find it.'

'The crossed sticks!' Tristan interrupted. He was sure they hadn't been at the entrance this morning. Lance and Leonora must have marked it. He raced back down the tunnel.

'They know you've found something,' Tiffany went on. 'They're coming back with gear so they can take it.'

'They wouldn't do that!' Nim exclaimed. 'They know the island's protected.'

'I heard them when they came back to the camp,' Tiffany said desperately. 'They want to destroy Jack's research, too. You've got to believe me, Nim.'

'But ...' Nim began.

'I've just worked something else out,' said Edmund. 'When we were on our way to the boat yesterday, Lance said, *Let's hope the cake was worth it*. Leonora told him to be quiet and changed the subject really fast – I think he'd forgotten I was in the back seat. But they must have been the scientist friends who gave Dr Ashburn and Professor Hunterstone a celebration dinner. What if they poisoned the cake?'

That's why Alex said, 'Ah!' like that when I said the Bijous were the same kinds of scientists, Nim thought. *She meant it reminded her of a plot for a mystery story!*

'That makes sense,' said Tiffany. 'They said all our parents were sweet and stupid.'

'Jack too?' asked Nim.

'They said he was so simple it was as if he wanted his research destroyed.'

Nim knew that Tiffany was telling the truth.

Tristan rushed back in. 'Lance and Leonora have stolen the boat! It's down in that little cove below us – and they're climbing the cliff. I was too late to move the sticks, they'd have seen me for sure.'

'We'll guard the tunnel,' Nim said fiercely. 'We're not letting them in!'

'We'll have to come out some time – and they've just hauled a big pack up here in pouring rain,' said Tristan. 'They're not going to go away just because we ask them to.'

'The way they said that nothing was going to stop them...' Tiffany shivered.

Ollie stared from one face to the other, and started to whimper. Fred scuttled back to Nim's shoulder.

Nim felt as if she'd swallowed a hurricane. Her thoughts whirled: she had to stop the Bijous, but she couldn't put everyone in danger; she had to stop them destroying Jack's research, but she had to guard the cave and the bats' nursery.

'We can't fight them while we've got Ollie,' said Tiffany, as if she'd read Nim's mind.

'But it's too late to run away,' said Tristan.

'The cavern has so many tunnels, there must be another way out,' said Nim. 'We can take Ollie somewhere safe and then I'll come back to...'

'I'll come back with you,' Edmund interrupted.

'So will I,' said Tris.

'I would if I could,' said Tiff.

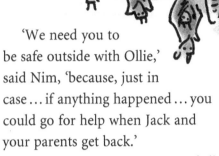

'We need you to
be safe outside with Ollie,'
said Nim, 'because, just in
case … if anything happened … you
could go for help when Jack and
your parents get back.'

That was the scariest thing of all.
Saying out loud that something could
go wrong meant it really could.

Nim led the others back through
the fossil tunnel and back into the main
cave. Silently, they tiptoed beneath the
dangling, sleeping bats, around the maze
of stalagmites, deeper and deeper into the
heart of the mountain. The glow-worms
disappeared: the dark was darker, the air was danker,
and the musty bat smell wasn't getting any weaker.

Maybe there isn't another way out, a voice whispered in
Nim's head. *Maybe you'll be trapped here forever.*

We're not trapped, she told it. *If we can't find another
tunnel we'll just go back. Lance and Leonora are scientists.
They're not going to hurt us.*

The dim glow from her headlamp shone into a
different darkness. She'd found another tunnel.

The floor was moist and slippery. It sloped downhill more steeply than the cave, and was deeper in the middle than the sides, as if it had been neatly hollowed out. *By water,* Nim thought. *This is the watercourse that comes out above Waterfall Cliffs!*

She was about to whisper the good news when the nasty little voice in her head said, *Or it's an underground creek that runs into an underground pool – and you'll never get out!*

Nim decided she wouldn't say anything yet.

'At least we can't get lost now,' Edmund whispered in her ear.

It was true. The tunnel was narrow and the only other openings were small nooks or alcoves, as if someone had thought about making a window or a door and then remembered that there was nowhere for it to go. All Nim had to do was keep on going, and all the others had to do was follow.

That didn't stop her stomach squirming with fear. Because even if they weren't exactly lost, they didn't know where they were, and they didn't know where Lance and Leonora were or what they were doing. And even though they were going as quickly as they could, it wasn't very fast because the tunnel was dark and the ceiling was low. Nim had to walk with her head bowed, and Edmund had to crouch. Ollie was the only one who could walk normally. He was still tied to Tiffany by the sleeping sheet, but he kept rushing ahead, sliding and bumping into Edmund.

Then they were all slipping, skidding down the tunnel. The floor was as slimy as a hungry slug, and so were the walls. They slid down as if they were going down the rainforest waterslide. It would have been fun if it hadn't been so dark and they hadn't been so scared of Leonora and Lance hearing them. But it was dark, and they were scared – all except Ollie.

'I'm going fast!' he squealed. 'Fast, fast, FAST!'

'SHH!' everyone else hissed.

But Ollie squealed and skidded again, passing Edmund and Nim, and Tiffany skidded behind him. Then his squeal changed to a screech, and there was a slithery crashing noise and a splash of pebbles into water, and then more crashing and a scream from Tiffany.

'Tiff!' Tristan shouted.

Tiffany and Ollie had disappeared.

Chapter 10

IN HER RAINFOREST STUDIO, Alex blinked and shook her head as if she was waking up from a nightmare. The hairs on her arms were prickling with her Hero's fear, because just as he was about to cut the fuse on the dynamite, he'd realised he didn't have a knife. He'd broken it cutting the Lady Hero free from the rock the Bad Guys had tied her to. So now he'd have to move the dynamite, and Alex wouldn't know for sure that he'd escape until she'd worked out exactly how long it would take him to run from the temple. She couldn't do that until she'd timed Nim running.

And she couldn't do that till Nim got away from the visiting scientists.

Alex shook her head again, and as if the last piece in a jigsaw puzzle had been shaken into the right space, she knew what had been bothering her. When Nim and Jack had told her about Selina Ashburn and Peter Husterstone becoming ill and Leonora and Lance stepping into their places, she'd thought it sounded like a plot from one of her stories.

Sometimes make-believe stories turn out to be a little bit true.

Leonora and Lance Bijou, Alex typed into her search engine.

The screen filled with a long list of articles.

As Alex read each heading, the hairs on her arms prickled harder. When she opened the first one, the hairs stood straight up.

Questions Surround Mystery Disappearance of Scientist

A geological expedition has come to a murky end after one of the scientists disappeared without trace. George Brown, a geologist, was working with palaeontologist Dr Leonora Bijou and her engineer husband Lance, when the team unearthed what was thought to be the biggest ruby ever found.

'Palaeontologist and engineer!' Alex exclaimed. 'They told Jack they were a biologist and geologist.'

Dr Brown disappeared two nights after the rare gem was discovered and hasn't been seen since. The ruby has also vanished.

'It's tragic,' Leonora Bijou said. 'We trusted this man, and it appears that he's betrayed us and run away with the jewel.'

Lance Bijou stated, 'Our interest was in the science of how this ruby could have formed, but it was also an extremely valuable gem. It seems that Dr Brown was more interested in the money than the science.'

The story was from a year ago. Below it was another article from the year before that.

Doubts about New Fossil Discovery

A week ago palaeontologist Dr Leonora Bijou discovered a rare fossil fish in an area where no fossils have been discovered before.

'This is a very exciting discovery,' a university spokesman said at the time. 'This species of fish live in fresh water, and this is the first proof that there was fresh water in this area in the Palaeozoic Era.'

The fossil has been named the Leonora Lungfish in Dr Bijou's honour.

However, Professor Maguire, from the university's palaeontology department, claims that the fossil had been stolen from his office two weeks earlier. 'I discovered this fossil myself, many years ago, in a well-known lungfish fossil site,' he stated.

Dr Bijou was highly indignant at these charges and has vehemently denied their truth. 'Professor Maguire is lying because he's jealous,' she said.

'My wife has proved that she's the best palaeontologist in the world,' Lance Bijou claimed. 'It's not surprising that other scientists resent her discoveries.'

We tried to interview Professor Maguire again, but unfortunately he was unable to speak to us due to a sudden illness.

There were lots more stories, but when Alex saw the words *sudden illness*, she knew she'd read enough.

'I was right,' she said out loud. 'This time the bad guys *are* real.'

She remembered how excited Nim had been this morning when they met on the trail, as if she was buzzing with a brand-new secret. Alex had a terrible feeling that the secret was something that could make Leonora Bijou very happy.

Nim was in danger.

'HELP! WE'RE DOWN here!' Tiffany's voice echoed up, high and quivery, from a hole in the tunnel floor.

Tristan had already thrown himself down beside it, wiggling so far into the shaft that Nim thought he was going to fall in too. She grabbed his right leg and Edmund grabbed the other.

The hole was shaped like a funnel and dropped straight down into the mountain. The mouth was wide, and the walls were slippery and smooth, polished by centuries of running water. Tiffany was jammed halfway down, where the walls narrowed so that she could brace one foot against each side of the wall. Ollie was hanging below her.

'Want to get out now!' they heard him whimper.

'We'll get you out,' Nim promised. She didn't know how, but they had to – they would!

Tristan slid further down into the funnel's mouth.

'We've got to get Ollie out first,' Tiffany hissed. 'He can't reach the sides – if the sheet tears…'

Nim and Edmund pulled Tristan back up. He was heavier than he looked.

'I can't see!' Tiffany shouted. 'I've lost my torch!'

Tristan leaned in again and dropped his down to her. It thumped against the wall, clattered and banged.

'Ouch!' Tiffany squeaked, and then there was a splash.

'Sorry!' said Tristan. His voice choked.

'Are you in water?' Nim called.

'It's below us,' Tiffany shouted.

'Wet toes,' Ollie sobbed.

Nim leaned over the hole so that her headlamp shone onto Tiffany. Edmund did the same.

With her legs jammed against the walls, Tiffany was hauling Ollie up by the sheet that tied them together. 'Climb like a monkey,' she was telling him, and Ollie stopped whimpering.

'Come on, Monkey Ollie!' Tristan called, and Ollie grabbed the sheet above his head.

Tiffany squatted, caught her little brother by the hands, and hauled him up between her knees. Tears glistened on her cheeks as she hugged him.

'You've still got to be a baby monkey,' she told him. 'Hold on tight while I untie my end of the sheet.'

'Don't untie it!' everyone shouted at once.

'I have to,' said Tiffany. Something in her voice stopped them from arguing.

But the knot around her waist had pulled tight. She tugged at the knot; her hand slipped and whacked hard against the rock. Ollie whimpered as if he was the one who'd been hurt, but Tiffany hardly seemed to notice. 'I can't untie it!' she grunted.

Nim felt as if she was going to burst. She wanted to climb down the shaft and do something, but all she could do was to angle her headlamp for the best light, holding her head still while her mind whirled. *If I could just lower her my pocketknife . . . But the cord's too short; it'll fall down past her like Tristan's torch.*

She pushed back from the edge and slipped the three cords off her neck. They'd never been untied, not since Jack gave her each one when she was a little girl – the shell whistle, then the spyglass, and finally, when she was old enough to be careful and strong enough to use it, the fat red pocketknife. The knots were like rock now; she opened the knife, sliced through each knot and pulled out the cords. She tied the ends of the first two together in a reef knot, hearing Jack's voice in her ears: *right over left and under, left over right and under* – and then tied the third cord onto the end the same way. Finally she closed the knife, slipped the cord through its ring and tied that too.

It seemed to take a long time, but when she finished, Tiffany was still struggling and the sheet was still knotted.

'I'm dropping you a knife!' Nim called. She leaned deep into the funnel the way Tristan had before. Tristan and Edmund grabbed her ankles.

The pocketknife swung on the long cord, clattering against the walls, and stopped, swaying above Tiffany's head. With Ollie clinging tight to her neck, Tiffany jammed her legs harder against the sides and reached.

She could nearly touch it – it was so close she could feel the air moving above her fingers as it swung – she tried again. And again and again, over and over ...

'I can't! I just can't.'

'I can!' Ollie squealed.

He clutched a handful of his sister's hair and pulled himself up to stand on her shoulders. Tiffany grabbed his feet, and the little boy stretched for the swinging knife.

'Got it!' he shouted triumphantly.

'Sit down on my shoulders while I use it,' said Tiffany. 'I don't want to cut your legs by mistake.'

Ollie handed her the knife and sat down obediently. Tiffany shoved the knife into the tight knot of the sheet.

Edmund and Nim aimed their lights onto it.

'Cut towards the wall!' Nim called. Tiffany didn't look like someone who'd used a pocketknife much before.

'I'm stuck, not stupid!' Tiffany grunted. She pushed hard; there was a ripping sound – but the sheet stayed stuck in its knot.

'Are you cutting the sheet, Tiff?' asked Ollie.

'I'm trying!'

'That's naughty,' said Ollie. He sounded confused.

'Mum won't mind,' Tiffany panted, as she dug the knife into the knot one more time. There was another ripping sound. The knot loosened.

Tiffany dropped the knife into her pocket and tugged the sheet open.

'Pull Ollie up now!' she called. She tossed her end of the sheet up the shaft. They all leaned down to grab it, with Tristan down the hole as low as he could go and Nim and Edmund holding his ankles till their arms ached and their hands were so slippery with sweat they were afraid he'd slide right out.

The sheet fluttered up and billowed down, like a baby bird learning to fly. It was too soft and loose to throw straight up.

Nim looked at Fred. Fred looked back at Nim. Fred was greedy, but he was brave too, and sometimes he knew what Nim was thinking. She lifted him off her shoulder and held him close to her heart to warm him.

'Are you sure?' she asked him.

She opened her hands, and Fred scuttled down her legs to the mouth of the shaft.

Nim's breath was stuck in her throat. There were no more cords to tie onto him.

Ollie started to whimper again. Nim wondered how long Tiffany could go on holding him. She swallowed hard.

'Fred's on his way!' she called. 'Hold the sheet out in case he falls!'

Fred slid down the side of the tunnel, his claws gripping where he could. Nim could hardly bear to watch, but she couldn't shut her eyes either.

'Fred!' Ollie and Tiffany shouted together.

Then Fred was on Ollie's shoulder, sneezing with relief.

'Yuck!' said Ollie, and stopped crying.

Tiffany untied the cord from Nim's pocketknife and shoved the knife back in her pocket. She tied one end of the cord around the loose end of the sheet, and the other end around Fred's shoulders.

'Is that too tight?' she asked.

Fred tried. He could slide down Tiffany's arm, but when he tried to scramble up the walls of the tunnel, the thick cord rubbed against his armpits and made his front legs clumsy. He slipped, and Tiffany caught him just in time.

Nim could hardly breathe. Watching and doing nothing was the hardest thing she'd ever done.

'I need your tail, Ollie,' said Tiffany. She lifted the necklace over the boy's head and undid the clasp. The amber scorpion plummeted to the bottom of the shaft. But that wasn't the part that Tiffany wanted. Untying Fred's cord, she knotted the golden chain into a harness around the iguana's shoulders. Now the cord was tied to the loop right in the middle of his back, lying smoothly between his spikes.

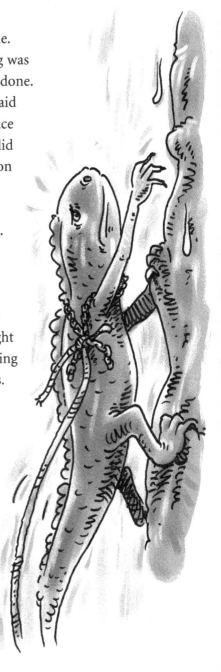

Fred raced across to the wall and started climbing back up to Nim, trailing the cord behind him. She dangled right down into the hole again, with the boys holding her ankles, because they all knew that Fred needed to see Nim to make him as brave and strong as he could be.

'You can do it, Fred,' Nim whispered.

Fred scuttled and scrambled, and pulled himself up those smooth funnel walls. His claws found every tiny crack and crevice that the water hadn't smoothed away. Sometimes he slipped down a little, but every time he started back up again and found a claw-hold that he'd missed before, and every time he ended up a bit higher than he'd been.

Finally he was close enough that Nim could touch his cool spiky back, then he crept up another lizard-length, and she could hold him in both hands. The boys dragged her back until she could sit up and untie Fred's golden harness.

Tristan grabbed the cord and started pulling the sheet up.

'Wait!' said Edmund. 'The cord's too thin – it'll slip right out of our hands once we're pulling Ollie. We need to wind it around something thicker.'

He dumped out his backpack and looked doubtfully at his paintbrush.

'My bottle!' said Nim. Her drinker was a thick piece of bamboo stem; it was strong and easy to hang onto. Tristan knotted the cord around the middle, threw himself back down on the floor and started hauling, winding the cord around the bamboo. Nim and Edmund held onto his feet.

'It's pulling!' Ollie screamed. 'I don't like it!'

Tristan had pulled in all the cord now; his hands were on the sheet.

'Kick off from the walls, Ollie!' he called, panting.

But Ollie was too terrified to push. His arms and legs were thrashing and waving like a fish trying to get free from a hook.

'Tris isn't going to be able to pull him in by himself,' Nim said.

Edmund nodded. It was as if they'd worked together forever. With a few smooth tugs, they hauled Tristan backwards.

'I can hold him myself now,' said Edmund.

Nim threw herself down on the floor beside Tristan and reached for the sheet. Ollie was close to the top. Another few hauls together and they'd be able to reach him.

There was a sharp ripping noise.

The terrified toddler was kicking and fighting so hard that he was tearing the knot in the sheet.

Tristan dived further into the shaft and grabbed his little brother's wrist. Then Edmund hauled Tristan, Nim hauled the sheet and Tristan hauled Ollie, and all four of them tumbled onto the floor like exhausted tug-of-war winners.

'Your turn, Tiff!' Tristan called when he could breathe again, untying Ollie from his sheet and dropping it back down to her.

'I can't,' said Tiffany. 'My foot's stuck in the rock.'

Chapter 11

TIFFANY'S WORDS EXPLODED over them. Time froze.

Then Tristan shouted, 'Of course you can get out! You have to.' Ollie started to sob, and Edmund pointed to a thin stream of water trickling down the tunnel towards them.

The rain that had started when Tiffany got to the cave was flowing all the way through from the entrance hole. There was already water below Tiffany. If more flowed in ...

Don't go down the shaft! Nim wished at the stream, but of course it did.

She looked at Edmund and could tell he was thinking the same thing.

'I know Lance and Leonora want to steal the fossil,' said Nim, 'but they'd *have* to help if we ask – they've got ropes and stuff, and they know about rocks. I'm going back to find them.'

'I'll go the other way,' Edmund said. 'It's definitely lighter ahead, and there are glow-worms again – we mustn't be far from the end of the tunnel. If I can get out that way, I can get back to camp for tools.'

'What if this fills up before you get back?' Tiffany shouted.

Which was exactly what they were all afraid of, and exactly what they didn't want her to think.

There was a long moment of silence. Long enough to hear that the drops plinking into the water had become a steady stream.

'We'll get you out before it does,' Tristan promised desperately.

Ollie started crying louder.

'We'll leave Tristan the backpacks,' Nim said. 'There might be something useful we've missed.'

Edmund took off his headlamp and gave that to Tristan too. Fred stopped hunting glow-worms and raced to Nim's shoulder. 'I'll be back soon!' she called. What she really wanted to say was, *I'm sorry I brought you here! I'm sorry I found the fossil and I'm sorry you fell down the hole even though I didn't know it was there, because it's my mountain and my tunnel and so it's my fault.* But that wouldn't make anything better right now. Right now they couldn't waste time worrying: they needed to act.

Because if that shaft filled up with water before they got Tiffany out, she would drown.

Ollie's crying grew to a wail.

'Take Ollie with you,' Tiffany shouted.

'No! Staying with Tris! Want Tiff to get out now!'

Edmund hesitated. The stream of water grew heavier. Ollie's wail grew to a scream.

Tristan stood up. Even in the darkness his expression looked torn. 'I'll go for help if Edmund will stay. Ollie, you're coming with me.' He handed the headlamp back to Edmund.

'Wait!' Nim shouted. 'If you can get out that way, follow the trail beside the creek. Alex Rover's studio is in the rainforest on the way to the house. She can use the satellite phone to call Jack. And she might have some ideas on how to get Tiffany out.'

'I need *real* help, not a storybook hero!' Tiffany shrieked.

'Alex Rover's here now?' asked Edmund.

'She's real and she's here,' said Nim. 'I'll explain later.'

She was pretty sure Alex would agree that keeping her secret wasn't as important as saving Tiffany.

There was only a narrow strip of floor around the edge of the hole. Nim waited to see Tristan and Ollie sidle safely around it, and then she started back up the tunnel the other way.

Edmund dumped out the backpacks, searching all over again for anything that could possibly help Tiffany get her foot out of the crack in the rock.

Tiffany stayed exactly where she was, listening to the water run down the sides of the shaft into the pool below, and wondering how fast it would rise. It was already up to her left ankle.

LEADING OLLIE BY the hand, Tristan felt his way down the tunnel. It was true that there was a tinge of grey ahead in the blackness, and the dancing blue lights of glow-worms, but they weren't enough to show him where the tunnel led, or if there was another giant hole ahead. So he slid his feet along the floor and patted his free hand along the walls, while part of him screamed, *Hurry up and save your sister!* and another part – one that didn't want to die falling down a hole inside a mountain – screamed, *Careful, go slow!*

The floor was smooth, but not wet-slippery: the water was all going down the shaft where Tiffany was stuck.

'But it's probably leaking out somewhere,' he told himself. 'And the rain's probably stopped now anyway.'

The tunnel curved and the slope became steeper. The roof was lower and the light brighter. Tristan put Ollie on his lap and skidded on his bottom like a kid on a slippery slide, around a curve and out into fresh air and rain.

The rain was coming down in bucketfuls. It splashed off rocks and turned dirt to mud. It gathered up Tristan and his little brother and swooshed them down the hill on the wildest, craziest ride of their lives.

They landed with a jolt on an arch of rock beside a waterfall. Tristan's heart slowed its thumping, and he rolled to his knees to look over the edge.

Far below was the pond Edmund had taken a picture of yesterday. 'It looks much prettier when you're not falling into it!' Nim had said.

So now there were two worst things that could happen. His little brother could fall off the cliff and drown. And his sister could stay stuck deep inside the cliff and drown.

Because the other thing Nim had said was that
a waterfall came out of the tunnel when it rained.
Rain was pouring into the start of the tunnel
now, but it wasn't flowing out this end yet.
First it had to fill in every hole along the way.
Including the one Tiffany was stuck in.

Tristan's heart began pounding again.
As if he was the one stuck in the shaft,
he felt darkness surrounding him, the
rock closing him in, his body crushed
by pain and terror.

It took all his strength to break free of that link. But if he was going to save his sister, he had to save himself first. And he was stuck halfway down a cliff, on a narrow bridge of rock, with an exhausted toddler in his arms.

NIM CREPT STEADILY up the tunnel, trying to keep to the edges where it was drier and not so slippery. Her headlamp glowed dimly; the trickling water was the only sound.

'I'm glad you're with me, Fred,' she said, as he rubbed his spiny back against her neck. Fred pressed a little closer. He loved sunshine and being able to move fast when his blood warmed up, but he loved Nim more.

'We don't need to be quiet,' Nim reminded him. 'It's okay if Lance and Leonora hear us now.'

Fred sneezed.

'Truly. They'll help us when I tell them what's happened.'

But her voice still came out in a whisper.

Besides, it was easier to be quiet so she could concentrate on climbing up the tunnel without slipping backwards or falling down any other holes. She didn't know how long she'd been climbing, and she didn't know how long it had taken them to go down in the first place. Now there was another tunnel shooting off from the side. She was sure she was still in the right one, but not one hundred per cent sure.

And she had no idea how close she was to the cave. Or what she'd do if Lance and Leonora had already gone.

Go to the Emergency Cave. There was rope there, and tools. Maybe she should have gone there in the first place. All she'd thought about was getting Tiffany and Ollie out right away.

She came to another side tunnel, and then another, and now she knew for sure that she was in the right tunnel and that it wasn't far to the bats' nursery cave.

She could hear voices: Leonora's, and then Lance's.

Nim remembered Leonora's smile, and the way that she'd listened to everything Nim had to say last night. Everything was going to be all right.

'Help!' she started to call.

Then she heard what they were saying, and the 'Help!' slipped back down her throat as quickly as a chunk of coconut into Fred's stomach.

'Careful!' said Leonora's voice. 'We don't want it to blow up too soon!'

Blow up? thought Nim, creeping closer.

'Don't worry – I won't light the fuse till we're out.'

'Are you sure that's the best place?'

'Perfect!' said Lance. 'When it collapses this cave it'll blow out the wall between here and the opal. No more stinky bats to worry about – and you'll have all the room you want to cut out that whole fossil.'

'The most perfect fossilised sea turtle ever found! I'll be famous!'

'Or we could break it into bits and sell the opals. There are some valuable pieces in there.'

'Rich or famous – we can't lose!' Leonora gloated.

Oh, yes you can! Nim wanted to shout.

'Okay, it's set!' said Lance. 'Let's get out quick. Three minutes till BOOM time, and this cave is dust. Bye, bye, bats!'

'Good riddance to the filthy things!' Leonora said, her voice disappearing as she scurried out through the door hole.

They're going to kill the bats! Nim's mind screamed. *And if I don't get out of here, they're going to kill me too.*

Lance said three minutes, said a calmer part of her mind. *All you have to do is cut the fuse. The dynamite can't go off if the spark doesn't get there.*

'Hang on, Fred,' she whispered. Fred clung to her shoulder a little tighter, and she crept the last three steps into the nursery cave. Her headlamp swooped around, lighting up the sleeping bats, the dripping stalactites and the pillars of stalagmite, the green-glowing fungi and the blue swinging glow-worms. It wasn't just a home to one of the world's most endangered species, it was a magical, geological, biological wonderland. And it was part of her island. It was not going to be destroyed.

Nim stepped into the middle of the cave and finally saw the dynamite. It was beside the stalagmite at the entrance to the fossil tunnel. Six little sticks, tied in a bundle, with a long rope of fuse leading out of the cave.

They looked just like they did in pictures, except they were horribly, dangerously real: six little sticks of evil. She didn't want to touch them.

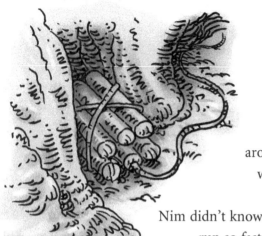

She reached for her knife – and then she remembered. The pocketknife wasn't around her neck. It was with Tiffany in a hole filling up with water. Nim didn't know that her brain could run so fast in so many different directions while her body was frozen in fear. She couldn't run far enough down the tunnel in three minutes to be safe.

Lance and Leonora weren't going to help her save Tiffany.

When the cave blew up the mother and baby bats in the nursery would all die and the bats would become extinct.

Alex Rover's Hero would pick up the dynamite and throw it down the cliff.

If the bat cave exploded, the start of the tunnel would fill up with rocks.

Tiffany was going to drown unless she stopped the rainwater from flowing down the tunnel into the shaft.

The only way to stop the water was to block the tunnel. The only way to block the tunnel was with a rockfall. And the only way to have a rockfall in just the right place…

If she threw the dynamite out to save the bats she'd be killing Tiffany.

Chapter 12

DEEP IN THE tunnel, Tiffany was struggling not to slide any further down the dark shaft. Her body was bruised and exhausted. She was cold, and she knew that she was probably still very, very scared. She was just too tired to feel the fear any longer.

It was her left foot that was stuck. It had slipped into the gap between two rocks as she fell and saved her from falling all the way down. At first she'd thought it was just a little bit stuck, and that she'd be able to pull it out when she wasn't holding Ollie. But her sneaker had wedged itself in further when she was stretching to reach Nim's dangling pocketknife, and that was when it had got jammed. The foot that had saved her was stopping her from getting out.

Now water had come up as high as her right ankle. Soon her stuck left foot would be underwater too, and she didn't know why that would make it worse, but it would.

'Can't you get your foot out of your shoe?' Edmund shouted.

'I've *tried!*'

TRISTAN WAS STUDYING the best way to get off the cliff.

'Don't move!' he ordered Ollie. He lay on his stomach and wiggled further out onto the rock bridge. Through the pouring rain, he could see the creek that Nim had told him to follow.

There was only one possible way to get there.

'You want to help get Tiff out of the hole?' he asked Ollie.

The little boy sniffed and nodded.

'We're going to crawl over this bridge.'

'Crawl like puppies?'

'Like snakes,' said Tristan. 'Flat on our tummies. You go in front.'

''Cause I'm the fastest,' said Ollie.

So I can grab you if you slip! 'Yes,' said Tris.

Ollie was right, though: it wasn't as long since he'd been crawling for real, and he was very good at it.

Tristan hated it. It hurt, it was scary, and it was very, very slow.

The bridge was quite flat on the top, and Tristan thought that on a sunny day it would be good to sit there and watch the waterfall splash past. But the rain was beating at their backs and pooling on the bridge so that sometimes it felt more like swimming than crawling, and the waterfall sent up plumes of spray that splashed into their eyes. Wriggle by wriggle, they slithered across.

Then: 'Hang on!' Tristan started to shout, but before he could finish the rain whooshed them down the other side of the arch, and they were rolling on the soft, soggy bank of the creek.

Tristan jumped to his feet. Ollie was still lying on the ground, looking as if he didn't know whether or not to cry.

'That was fun!' Tristan told him.

'Fun,' Ollie repeated, not sounding too sure.

'Want a piggy back?' Tristan picked his brother up, and started down the creek.

He'd never have believed how fast he could run around rocks, through pouring rain and slippery mud, with a three-year-old on his back. He could hear himself puffing; he could see blood from the scratches on his arms, but he couldn't feel the pain, the rain, or his heaving chest. All he saw was the best possible path in front of him, and all he heard was the chant in his head, *Follow the creek, follow the creek to the house, follow the creek to rescue Tiff.*

NIM HAD BEEN afraid many times in her life. She'd been nervous when she rode Selkie out to sea to rescue Alex

Rover. She'd been scared when she dived off the cliff to rescue Selkie. But she'd never been terrified like this.

She grabbed her whistle from her pocket and blew three loud blasts under the sleeping bats. The air filled instantly with a chirping, flapping cloud. But instead of heading towards the door hole, the bats were disappearing down the long tunnel, the way Nim had just come. They were flying fast.

'Oh, no!' Nim groaned, 'I've confused them!'

Or maybe they were going out the way they always did. At the back of Nim's mind things started to fall into place: why she'd never seen any bat poo outside the door hole on the Black Rocks, and why the tunnel had smelled of bats all the way down.

Now she had to make sure they had a nursery to come home to again.

She picked up the bundle of dynamite. It was heavier than it looked, but the hardest thing was making sure she didn't trip on its snaking fuse. She wanted to run, but she didn't want to fall.

'Get down and get out!' she ordered Fred. 'What if I've worked out the time wrong?'

Fred dug his claws in deeper. He never liked Nim telling him what to do, especially if it meant leaving her. And most especially if it meant leaving her in danger.

Nim didn't have time to argue. She rushed down the side tunnel to the turtle fossil. As gently as if were a clutch of newly laid eggs, she laid the dynamite at the bottom of the wall, under the gleaming fossil of Chica's millions-of-great-great-grandmother.

The fossil was beautiful; it told a fascinating story of history and geology – but the turtle had died a long time ago. Tiffany and the bats were alive now.

Sacrificing the fossil was the only possible way to save them both.

Nim raced back out, around the stalagmite, through the entrance passage, and slid out the opening into a deluge of rain.

Fred leapt off her shoulder and somersaulted with her down the hill. They were still rolling when they heard the boom. Nim pressed her hands over her ears so tightly her jaws hurt, but she couldn't stop herself from watching.

A spray of fiery, glistening opals shot out over the cliff. Like a rainbow cloud in the rain, it hung in the air for a moment before disappearing down to the sea.

CAUTIOUSLY, NIM LOOSENED her hands from her ears. Fred pulled his head out from under her arm. They heard the thump of one last rock and the drumming of rain... and then a desperate, raging howl from somewhere below.

'My fossil!' Leonora roared. 'My opals! You set the dynamite in the wrong place!'

'No, I didn't!' Lance bellowed back.

Nim hated even hearing their voices. She hated the thought of ever seeing them again. But she had to give it one more try.

'Leonora,' she called. 'Lance! HELP!'

'We've got to get out of here,' she heard Lance shout.

There were crashes of panicky skidding and loose stones bouncing down the Black Rocks, then even that noise was swallowed by the pouring rain.

Nim couldn't waste time chasing them. She couldn't waste energy being angry. She needed all the time and energy she had to rescue Tiffany.

Fred scuttled to her shoulder as she raced back up the hill. 'We don't need them,' she told him. 'If we get some tools we can do it ourselves.'

She said it again and it sounded a bit better. She was almost ready to believe it by the time she reached the tree that had hidden the cave's entrance for so many years.

The tree was lying across the path, its top branches dangling over the cliff, its roots in the air. Nim felt smaller than pond algae. 'Sorry, tree,' she said.

But then she looked at where the door hole used to be, and felt as if she could soar higher than a frigate bird. There was no door, no hole at all, just a solid wall of rocks. Her plan had worked: the rock wall was stopping the rain from running through the cave into Tiffany's tunnel.

Now they just needed to get her out.

Nim rushed back down to the Emergency Cave. Lance and Leonora's tool bag was in the doorway, with a coil of rope on top. Nim strapped the bag to her back, slung the rope over the shoulder that Fred wasn't sitting on, and started the long way round to the waterfall.

She whistled for Selkie as she ran. She didn't know where Selkie was or what a sea lion could do to help. But Selkie was very strong, and smart in a different way to people-smart – and Nim was going to need all the help she could get.

SELKIE HAD WAITED a long time after Lance and Leonora disappeared up the cliff. She tried fishing for a while and she dozed for a bit, but whatever she did she listened for Nim. She was getting anxious, and she was getting bored.

The more bored she was, the more interesting the rubber dinghy seemed. Selkie had never seen a rubber dinghy on the Black Rocks before. As the rain started, she flopped up the rocks and into the dinghy. With a little shove of her tail and a wiggle of her body, she rode it like a toboggan, all the way down to the water.

For a few minutes, she rode the dinghy around the cove, barking happily. If Leonora and Lance had known anything about sea lions, they would have come running.

But they didn't, and so they didn't see the sad end to Ryan and Anika's rubber dinghy.

Because rubber dinghies aren't toboggans. They're not supposed to be ridden over sharp rocks by sea lions that weigh as much as two men. So the air hissed slowly out of the cuts in the rubber dinghy's bottom, and Selkie floated around going slowly deeper and deeper until she disappeared right under the water.

The sea lion bobbed back up from the cove's stony floor, but the dinghy didn't.

Selkie honked in a way that might have been a bad word if she'd been a person. It had been fun having her own boat.

The fishing boat was still there, bobbing on its anchor. She was just circling it, searching for the easiest way up, when the world shook with a terrible *boom!*

Selkie bounced out of the water, straight onto the boat. She was still shaking her head to get the noise out when Leonora and Lance came skidding down the rocks.

'Where's the dinghy?' Leonora shrieked. 'We've got to get out of here before Jack gets back!'

'We'll have to swim,' said Lance.

Selkie didn't care anymore that Nim and Jack had let these people onto the island. The world wasn't supposed to *boom!* and people weren't supposed to shout. She barked a warning.

Lance dived off the rocks.

Selkie dived off the boat.

They met nose to nose under the water. Selkie's nose was bigger, and so were her teeth. Lance shot out of the water – but he still wasn't safe. Barking and honking, Selkie chased Leonora and Lance up off the rocks and deep into the rainforest, as far from the camp as she could push them. They were soaked to the skin, too exhausted to run any further, and too afraid to understand that the terrifying sea lion had gone on past and left them alone. When they did get brave enough to make their way back out into the pouring rain and jungle mud, they were absolutely, completely, spun-around-in-circles lost.

Chapter 13

THE *BOOM!* ECHOED deep into the heart of the mountain. Edmund felt the tunnel floor tremble.

'Are you okay?' he called.

'What was that?' Tiff shouted at the same time.

Then the air filled with strange, clicking chirps and a scent of musk, and a long thin cloud of bats flew down the tunnel. They flew over Edmund's head, over Tiffany in the shaft, and out to the world on the other side.

Tiffany's going to freak out for sure, Edmund thought. *And I don't blame her!*

'Are you okay?' he called again.

'That was beautiful!' Tiff called back. She sounded stronger than she had since Tris and Ollie had left. 'If they can get out, I can too.'

NIM LOVED THE rainforest on sunny days. It stayed cool and shady no matter how hot it was everywhere else. Vines trailed from branches, and trees with great walls of roots made secret nooks and grottos. Invisible birds sang among the leaves, and then flew past in explosions of colour.

There were tiny green tree frogs, colour-changing lizards and whole universes of insects.

She loved the rain too, because nothing could live without it, but she loved rain a whole lot more when she wasn't in it. Her squelching shoes were getting heavier with each muddy step, and water was blurring her eyes. Her foot was skidding on a slippery root and a loop of vine was catching her leg...

Nim crashed face first into the mud.

'OW!' she screamed, and then, 'Fred?'

Fred scuttled up to her. He had leapt off her shoulder just in time.

'Sorry, Fred,' said Nim, kissing the top of his spiny head. She put him back on her shoulder; Fred was too chilled to run by himself now. 'I'll be more careful,' she promised. Her left knee throbbed and she rubbed it till it felt good enough to stand on. She thought the other knee was bleeding, but there was too much mud to be sure.

She didn't care about falling in the mud, but she did care about hurting Fred. And if she sprained her ankle or smashed her knee she wouldn't be able to rescue anyone.

TIFFANY COULDN'T FEEL her left foot anymore. She knew it must still be there, stuck through the crack, but it was completely numb. Worse, her arms and right leg were shaking with strain. She didn't know how long she could keep on pressing against the walls to hold herself up.

'Talk to me!' she called.

'No more water's coming down the tunnel,' said Edmund, but it was the fifth time he'd told her that, and it didn't sound as hopeful as it had at first.

He started going through the daypacks again, just in case he'd missed something that could possibly help. It was better than doing nothing. He knew he couldn't do anything without the ropes and climbing gear – but he didn't know how long he could just sit and wait for them.

'Do you remember the story in *Winnie the Pooh*?' he asked. 'When Pooh gets stuck in Rabbit's door and Rabbit reads him stories till he's thin enough to get out?'

Tiffany made a strange sort of sound. Edmund couldn't tell if she was laughing or crying.

'I'm going to see if anyone's coming yet,' he called. 'Don't go away! I mean … I'll be right back!'

Scuttling down the dark tunnel like a skater bug, he skidded around the curve towards the pale light of the outside world. He slid faster until one leg shot into

nothing, and caught himself just before he whooshed right down the hill.

He peered out into the rain like a turtle poking its head out of its shell. Below the muddy hill, he could see the cliffs he'd fallen off last time, and the pond he'd landed in. There was the rock bridge too, but some of it was narrow and all of it was high and he didn't know how Tristan could have crossed it with Ollie. Edmund shuddered and peered out further.

All he could see was green: trees and bushes and whatever else was hiding in the rainforest. 'Nim!' Edmund shouted. 'NIM!'

His voice was puny against the thunder of the waterfall and rain. There was no answer.

He slid back into the tunnel and the darkness. 'They'll be coming soon, Tiffany,' he called as he came back around the bend.

There was no answer here either.

Edmund rushed to the edge of the hole. 'Tiff!' he shouted. 'Are you okay?'

He knew it was a silly question, but he needed to hear her say something. Anything – even if it was just to tell him he was being stupid.

When she still didn't answer he knew that now she was really not okay.

SOMEONE WAS CRASHING through the forest below Nim.

I hope it's not Leonora and Lance! she thought.

The crashing came closer – and Selkie galumphed out from the trees. For a long moment, Nim hugged Selkie and Selkie whuffled over Nim – and right in the middle of that hugging, whuffling moment, the rain stopped. The sun came out and sparkled diamonds on the wet leaves and dripped hope through the branches. Nim shook out her wet hair, picked up the heavy coil of rope that had slipped off her shoulder, and they started off again, as fast as they could through the mud.

Five minutes later they reached the pond at the bottom of Waterfall Cliffs. Nim stared across at the great rock bridge arching over it to the cliff.

'What if we get all the way up there and we're in the wrong place?' she said.

Selkie nuzzled her, telling her that everything would be all right. Sometimes Selkie forgot that Nim wasn't a little sea lion pup whose problems could be fixed with nuzzles and love. She didn't know that the only thing that mattered was getting to Tiffany in time, and they couldn't do that if they couldn't find the tunnel.

Nim looked up, but they were too close under the cliffs to see to the top. She hurried on around the edge of the pond, past the main bats' cave. A few bats were flying confusedly in front of the entrance as if they were trying to decide whether or not to go in. When Nim looked more carefully, she could see the baby bats clinging to their mothers.

'They got out in time!'

Except that there weren't very many bats here, and there'd been more than she could count in the nursery cave.

'Maybe they've already settled further into this cave. Selkie, you go in and check – it might go deeper than we realised. I'm going over the bridge.'

Selkie honked crossly.

'I'll be right above you once I find the tunnel,' said Nim. 'We'll just have mountain in between us.'

'HMPHH!' Selkie snorted, even more crossly, but she knew she couldn't climb the great rock arch. She lolloped slowly into the cave as Nim started around the pond.

FROM THE BASE of the bridge, Nim could see to the top of Waterfall Cliffs. Water was trickling from every hole and crack in the rock so that the whole cliff face was sparkling in the sun. It would have been beautiful if she hadn't known that all that water had run deep through mountain tunnels to get there.

She stared up higher, past where the bridge met the wall, past the waterfall and up to the muddy hill above it, wet and shining in the sun. She could see the hole where the extra waterfall sometimes flowed, but there was no water coming out of it now.

Instead, a cloud of bats was going in.

'That *is* the tunnel! Nim exclaimed, and danced Fred in the air till he sneezed.

In the time since Nim had left Tiffany, she'd trekked the long way back through the tunnel, been as terrified as anyone could be, moved a bundle of dynamite, rolled down a hill, climbed back up the Black Rocks and carried a heavy pack and rope around another hill through the rainforest. A second ago she'd been so tired she didn't know how she could climb to the top of the bridge.

Now she was as full of energy as Fred eating coconut on a hot day. She tightened the straps on Lance's pack, told Fred to hold tight, and started up the arch.

On one side was the thundering waterfall; on the left she could see the creek meandering through the trees. But now she was imagining Tristan trying to carry his little brother along it, and the creek had never seemed so rushing, or the rocks so big. Tristan mightn't have found Alex yet. She didn't even know if he and Ollie had got out of the tunnel safely.

EDMUND STARED DOWN into the pit. Tiffany was still straddled across it, but her head was hanging as if she was asleep. Edmund called to her, quietly at first and then louder.

Tiffany didn't move.

Edmund stuffed the sheet and Nim's pack inside his own, and slipped it on his back. He knew that every single rock-climbing guide in the world would say that without a rope or climbing gear, he shouldn't do what he was going to do.

He had to do it.

He slid his legs down into the shaft, then his body, and finally he was clinging to the top with just his hands. Letting go was the hardest thing he'd ever done, but one foot found a crack to hang onto and the other a bump to step on ... and he was propped against the walls the same way as Tiffany, except that both his feet were free to slide down to the next bump and crack.

He slid and gripped, steadied himself and slid again. His right leg first and then his left; his right arm found a new grip and the left arm found one too.

The left foot found a bump ...

'My hand!' Tiffany screamed.

Edmund jumped off fast. So fast that he skidded right past her, down the smooth, sloping walls and into the water.

Tiffany screamed; Edmund gasped, gurgled, and sank. He kicked and thrashed, but the walls were slippery and the shaft was narrow, so he went on down. *I'm going to drown! Tiffany's held on all this time and I'm going to drown as soon as I try to help her!*

His feet touched rock. Edmund kicked off as hard as he could and shot up to the surface. He grabbed the wall and braced, spluttering and coughing.

There was a gurgling sound, and a rush of running water.

'The water's draining!' Tiffany exclaimed. 'How did you do that?'

'I guess I kicked the plug out,' said Edmund.

They could hear the water splashing onto a puddle, somewhere far below – *in another tunnel, or a cave,* Edmund thought, though he wasn't sure if that was good news or not.

And his headlamp was waterproof. That was the best surprise all day. He shone it down the shaft as the last swirl of water drained away.

'Thanks,' said Tiffany. 'My leg was going numb in the water. But for a minute I thought you were going to drown!'

'So did I,' admitted Edmund.

But Tiffany was still just as stuck as she'd been before. Edmund braced himself and shone his light on the rock that was trapping her foot. It looked like another loose rock that had washed down and got jammed in the crack in the wall. He'd kicked out the rock that blocked the drain; surely he could pull this one out too...

He tugged, yanked, pushed and grunted. The rock didn't budge.

There was another crack in the wall just above it, with a strip of rock going across from one side to the other like the bar of an H. Edmund had another idea. He shrugged off his dripping backpack and pulled out Nim's empty pack and the sheet.

FROM THE TOP of the rock arch, Nim was looking down at the deep blue pond. She was a very long way up, and the bridge was slippery with waterfall spray. Then she thought about Tristan and Ollie trying to cross it in pouring rain, and crawled quickly the rest of the way across.

The rock was almost flat where the arch joined the cliff. So much mud washed down to it with each rain that tough, straggly bushes were growing on it, the only bit of green on the harsh grey rocks. It was a good place to catch her breath.

Above the waterfall it was hill more than cliff; mud more than rock. Mud is easy to slide down, but hard to climb up. 'There's nothing else you can do,' she told herself sternly.

She was just about to start climbing when she heard a faint voice.

'You're crazy!'

Which was exactly what Nim was thinking, but the voice wasn't in her head. It was in the mountain – and so was the voice that answered.

'Maybe. But if it's strong enough to hold me it'll hold you.'

'Edmund?' Nim called.

'That's weird,' she heard. 'It sounded like Nim.'

'It's coming from the crack where my foot's stuck,' said Tiffany.

'I'm on the bridge!' Nim shouted.

She pushed through the bushes till she found a hole leading into the cliff. Nim crouched and leaned in.

'Can you hear me?' she shouted, just as Edmund's voice floated out, 'Can you hear us?'

Nim really didn't want to climb into another tunnel that she didn't know, but the opening was wide, and she could see a long way in. It slanted upwards, so she wasn't going to slide down anywhere except back to this safe flat patch. And she knew that Tiffany and Edmund were very close, at the other end of it. Though if the end was a crack small enough to trap Tiffany's foot, Nim wasn't going to fit through from this side.

Fred had already jumped off her shoulder and started in. Nim pulled on her headlamp and crawled after him.

The tunnel ended in a small cavern, tall enough for Nim to stand straight, but with water up to her knees.

Inside the shaft, light glimmered through cracks in the wall.

'Look!' Edmund called.

'We can see your light!' said Tiffany.

'And I can see yours,' Nim called back.

She sloshed through the water towards them. There were two strips of fabric across a bar of rock; when she got closer she saw they were the shoulder straps from a backpack – and when she looked through the crack above it she saw Tiffany swinging in a hammock seat.

'I tied the sheet through the pack's top handle, and wrapped it around with the cord,' said Edmund. 'It's pretty strong.'

'It's good,' said Tiffany. 'I couldn't have hung on much longer.'

Her voice was trembly and faint, and she was still anchored to the cliff wall by her left foot. Her sneaker toe was pointing through a crack into Nim's side of the cavern.

'Can you push it back?' Tiffany asked.

Gently at first, then harder, Nim tried to shove the sneaker through the crack. It didn't move.

'Try harder!' Tiffany said.

Nim pushed as hard as she could.

Tiffany screamed. Her foot still didn't move.

'Sorry!' Nim cried.

This was worse than ever. Now she'd actually hurt Tiffany as well as wasting time. She couldn't get through and she couldn't help from this side. She'd have to crawl back out and climb that steep, slippery hill with the rope and heavy pack on her back before she could even start to rescue Tiffany.

'Come on, Fred,' she called. Fred was trying to catch a glow-worm. He was balancing on the bar of rock with his tail poking towards her and his head in the shaft.

'Don't eat the lights!' Edmund exclaimed.

'No glow-worms, Fred,' Nim agreed. 'But great idea.' She lifted him out of the way and poked the end of the rope through the gap. There was only one rope, but it was very long. Edmund caught it and knotted it into a harness around his waist. Nim looped it securely around the bar. There was still a lot left.

Now to get Tiffany's foot free.

Nim searched through Lance and Leonora's tool bag. It had a first aid kit, two spikes for hammering into rock, a pulley and two cleats, a hammer and a small, neat parcel of fishing net.

'Why would they want a fishing net?' Nim wondered.

'To lower the fossil off the cliff,' said Tiffany.

'It wouldn't be much use the way the fossil is now,' said Nim. She wished she'd checked the backpack before carrying it all the way up here. This little spike and hammer were the only things she really needed ...

'Ow!' Tiffany screamed.

'I haven't hit anything yet!'

'It's a cramp in my other foot,' Tiffany groaned. 'I don't care if you hit this one – just get it out!'

Nim thought Tiff might care if the hammer did hit her, but she wedged the spike into the crack below the rock. She hammered and tapped, and then she stopped and Edmund tugged. The rock didn't move. Nim moved the spike, hammered and stopped again, Edmund tugged again, and the rock didn't move again.

This time she couldn't pull the spike out to move it. It was in too deep.

'Try the other spike,' said Edmund, but Nim was already swinging the hammer for one last try. She missed the spike and hit the rock hard. The rock tilted forwards and tumbled down the shaft bouncing off the rock walls, and right through the hole at the bottom ...

There was a splash, and a cross *Honk!*

Chapter 14

ALEX RAN OUT of her studio so fast she didn't have time to shut the door. She was running down the narrow path towards the trail to the house, faster than she'd ever known she could. Nim was in danger.

She was trying to think as she ran but Alex wasn't very good at doing two things at once, especially if one of them was running. *Get the satellite phone and call Jack to come home!* That was easy to think. So was *Keep Nim away from Leonora and Lance!*

The tricky part was that first, she had to find Nim. Or find Leonora and Lance and then work out how to keep them away from Nim.

Alex was thinking-and-running so hard that she didn't have time to look around when she reached the main trail. She didn't see the boy with a smaller boy on his back running as hard as he could up from the creek towards her.

Tristan skidded to a stop, Alex crashed into him, and they all tumbled to the ground. Luckily Ollie ended up on top.

'Are you Alex Rover?'

'Yes,' Alex gasped. She waited for the boy to say, 'But you're not a man!' Or: 'You've got the same name as the great adventure writer!'

'Tiffany needs help. We need our parents to come back now.'

Alex pointed towards the house. She was still panting too hard to speak, but she started running again. Tristan and Ollie followed.

'Sorry, Selkie!' Nim shouted.

'How did she get down there?' asked Edmund.

'She was checking out the bat cave,' said Nim. 'There's a big puddle inside it…that must be what's below this shaft.'

'So maybe we can get out that way too,' said Edmund.

'But I'm still stuck!' Tiffany shrieked, desperately trying to yank free. There was more room now that the top rock was gone, but her foot was so swollen that it was still stuck firm.

Nim stared at the sneaker toe sticking through to her side of the tunnel. Suddenly she had an idea. Inside the first aid kit there was a bottle of Leonora's soothing, slippery coconut oil.

She handed it through the window. As Edmund held the hammock steady, Tiffany reached for the bottle. Holding her breath to keep her hand from shaking, she trickled the oil down the crack into her sneaker.

When every drop was gone, she grabbed her leg just above her swollen ankle, pulled, twisted, and with a final yell, threw herself back into her hammock. Red and puffy, scraped and bloody, her foot popped out of its oily sneaker. 'I'm free!'

Tiffany reached through the gap and held Nim's hand; she held Edmund's hand with her other and Edmund held Nim's. It felt as if they were dancing in a circle, except that no one moved.

Then Fred sneezed, and from far below, Selkie barked sharply.

'We're coming!' Nim shouted.

But they still had to work out how. Tiffany was too weak and wounded to climb.

'I'll see if we can get down the shaft to where Selkie is,' said Edmund.

Nim loosened the rope tying him to the rock bar, and cleated it so he could lower himself a little way at a time instead of crashing to the bottom.

Edmund slithered down to the narrow part of the funnel. The opening was big enough for his feet to go through, but not the rest of him.

'Watch out, Selkie!' he shouted. Because it looked as if there were more loose rocks, like the one he'd kicked out when he was trying not to drown. He jumped and stamped; Nim checked that the rope was holding tight, and he jumped again.

A big rock broke free. They could hear it splash into the puddle at the bottom. A mini-avalanche of little ones plinked in after it.

'There's heaps of room now!' Edmund called up. Nim measured out more rope so he could go further.

Then Tiffany watched from her hammock, Nim and Fred watched through the gap, Selkie waited at the bottom and Edmund slipped down the rope till one foot touched water and the other touched sea lion.

He was in a knee-deep puddle of water in a far corner of the bat cave. Glow-worms danced all around him, bats hung upside down above him, and in front of him the pond sparkled deep and blue.

'We can do it!' he shouted. He rubbed Selkie's head thank you, and started back up the rope.

It wasn't as easy as sliding down. He walked his legs up the sides of the shaft and hauled himself up on the rope, with Nim cleating it in from the top so he didn't fall back down what he'd just climbed.

By the time he got there, Tiffany's foot looked like a balloon with toes. It didn't look like a foot that could brace itself against walls to climb down the shaft.

So they threaded the other end of the rope around her hammock and pulled it in tight till Tiffany was sitting up with her knees bent. They checked all the knots, tugged and pulled and checked again before they undid the backpack straps from the bar of rock.

Then with Edmund guiding the sheet-hammock as he slid down his own rope and Nim paying the hammock rope out through a pulley, they lowered Tiffany gently down the shaft to Selkie's waiting back.

THE SEA LION splashed gently forward until Tiffany could see the sky and the world beyond the cave. The water in the puddle was smelly, but Tiffany didn't care – it was cool on her swollen, oily ankle. She rested her face against Selkie's shoulder and felt her feet relax.

'All clear!' Edmund shouted up the shaft.

Nim untied the ends of the ropes. They snaked down with a splash.

That was when Tiffany realised that the water was getting warmer, fizzing and bubbling under her toes. 'That's weird!' she said, but Edmund had his head in the shaft, untangling a loop of rope caught on a rock, and didn't hear.

Tiffany was so tired she could hardly move, but she knew what she had to do. With trembling fingers, she reached for the water bottle on her belt.

High above, Nim had just finished packing up all the tools and extra bits when she noticed Tiffany's empty sneaker still poking into her cavern.

Nim pulled it through the crack, but it was so slippery with the coconut oil that it slipped right out of her fingers into the puddle she was standing in. The water was cool, and up past Nim's ankles, but she'd been in it for so long she'd forgotten about it.

By the time she'd fished the oily sneaker out, the water was fizzing and warm.

'How did that happen?' Nim exclaimed. Fred didn't have any answers but Nim searched quickly through the tool bag for a test tube, because she knew Jack would have questions.

There were no test tubes, or bottles, or anything else to take a sample. Nim didn't feel like exploring these tunnels and caves again for a very long time, but, 'We'll come back tomorrow,' she said.

Hoisting the tool bag onto her back, she crawled out of the tunnel and down the rock bridge.

Selkie dived across the pool to meet her, barking happily, but there was no time for long sniffs and whuffles. They raced around the pond.

Tiffany was waiting in front of the bat cave, her face lifted to the sun as she breathed in the warm fresh air.

But after Nim got out the first aid box and helped her clean and bandage her wounded ankle and foot, Tiff was even paler than before.

Edmund was staring down the creek. Nim knew what he was thinking: there was no way Tiffany could walk over these rocks.

But Selkie had other ideas. She was looking at Nim, and nudging Tiffany.

'Selkie wants you to ride her,' said Nim.

Tiffany let her breath out in a long sigh of relief and excitement. 'Truly?'

'Truly,' said Nim. She hugged Selkie for a moment, whispering, 'I'm so proud of you!' Tiffany handed her back the pocketknife, and Nim cut a piece of rope to loop around Selkie's shoulders so Tiffany could hold on. Sea lions are slippery when they galumph, even when they're not in the water.

That was when they heard a shout. 'Tiff!'

Tristan was running towards them, with Ollie and Alex Rover a little way behind.

There was so much hugging, laughing and so many babbled questions – as well as a little bit of crying – that it took a while for anyone to understand what anyone else was saying.

'Tiff's foot's too big,' said Ollie. 'It's yucky.'

'We need to get her back to the camp as fast as we can,' agreed Tristan. Tiffany was lying with her face on Selkie's neck, too tired to speak.

'She'll be better off at the house,' said Alex.

'The creek path is a long way for Tiffany to ride Selkie,' said Nim. 'It'll be faster to take the short cut back through the rainforest to the Black Rocks. Jack could pick us up there in the boat.'

'I don't know if he's got the message yet,' said Alex. 'He might be ages.'

'What would your Hero do?' Nim asked, because sometimes when things were bad, the only way she could work out what to do was to try to be an Alex Rover hero.

'You're Alex Rover?' Tiffany demanded. 'The real Alex Rover? I thought he was a man.'

'I'm the real one,' said Alex. 'I just made up the hero.'

'She's definitely real,' said Tristan.

Nim wasn't listening. Alex Rover's Hero moved fast and thought faster, but he never moved before he thought. He'd want to know exactly where he was, and exactly where everyone else was, before he went anywhere.

He'd climb a tree, like the one in front of her.

Nim grabbed a thick vine dangling off the huge tree, and swung hand over hand to climb the trunk. Through her spyglass, she could see a faint shape that could be Jack's sail. But when she looked again she thought it might be just a patch of sunlight on the waves – and whatever it was, it was very far away.

She wriggled partway around the trunk. From here the sea was a darker blue; she could see the Black Rocks, and the little cove at the bottom of the cliff ... and Ryan and Anika's wooden fishing boat.

'I wonder why Lance and Leonora didn't leave after I blew up the cave?' said Nim.

Selkie barked sharply, showing her teeth.

'You chased them away,' said Nim.

Selkie honked happily. Nim stroked her. She wished she knew where the Bijous were now, but the other thing Alex Rover's Hero always said was to only worry about one thing at a time. Right now, that one thing was getting Tiffany down to the boat and back to safety.

OUT ON THE reef, in the deep dark blue of the ocean, Jack pulled up his anchor and turned the sailboat towards the island. Anika and Ryan sighed, happy to have been there and sad to leave. A boat was so much more fun than a lab that they hadn't even minded the rain.

'I don't know if our research today will lead to a perfect biofuel,' said Anika. 'But I've seen corals that I never knew existed. As long as scientists keep on working together and discovering new things, we know there's hope for the future.'

Ryan gazed at his collection of neatly labelled test tubes. 'I've got enough research here for six months' work. Maybe something will lead us to that biofuel.'

'Or Leonora and Lance might have discovered the missing link,' said Jack.

'Or maybe the kids will,' said Anika. 'I wonder if they've had as good an adventure today as we have?'

The two men smiled with her. The white sails caught the wind and blew them towards the distant smudge of island.

SELKIE CARRIED TIFFANY over the curve of the rainforest to the trail past the caves. Tiffany had to lie on the sea lion's back, because her foot would have dragged on the ground if she'd sat up straight, but Selkie went so slowly and carefully that Tiffany never fell off.

But it was a long drop from the cliff to the cove, and Tiffany would fall off for sure if she tried to ride the sea lion down those huge steep rocks.

'I could slide,' said Tiffany.

'No,' said everyone else. They'd all seen Tiffany's face when her foot had bumped into things on the trail.

'Remember in *Passage to Patagonia*, when the tribe is carrying the wounded warrior through the jungle?' said Edmund.

'Perfect!' said Nim.

'I just made it up,' said Alex. 'I don't know if it'll work.'

With her pocketknife, Nim cut two lengths of thick, strong vines. They wove them through the ends of the fishing net to make handles.

Tiffany slid off Selkie's side onto the net. Tristan handed her their sleeping brother, and Tiffany wrapped her arms tight around him.

Then Nim and Edmund took the front handles, and Alex and Tristan took the back. Nim and Edmund clambered down the first rock, towing the stretcher behind them, while Alex and Tristan steadied, stretched and lowered it to them.

Boulder by boulder, balance by balance, they climbed on down.

They were just about halfway when they heard a noise. The sound of a boat engine starting.

There was nothing else it could be, but they went on hoping. There was nothing else they could do, so they kept on going.

But the boat was gone.

Chapter 15

THEY ALL SLUMPED onto the rocks. Taking the fishing boat back to the camp had seemed such a perfect idea that they hadn't worked out another one.

Tiffany slid off the stretcher and dozed on the rocks, still holding her sleeping brother on her stomach.

'What do we do now?' Tristan asked. He didn't really expect anyone to answer, and for a long time no one did. Because carrying Tiffany down a rocky cliff on a stretcher had been hard enough. Carrying her safely back up again, or over the crazy tumbled boulders of the Black Rocks, was impossible.

'We should have waited at the Emergency Cave,' Nim said. 'At least Tiff would have been out of the sun.'

Tiffany woke up at the word *cave*. 'Lance and Leonora talked about wrecking Jack's lab – what if they come back with more dynamite to blow up that cave too?'

'We've got to get Tiff out of here,' said Tristan. 'We'll just have to take her over the rocks on the stretcher.'

'Alex,' said Nim, 'do you remember the experiment you asked about the first time you wrote to Jack?'

'Of course I remember! It saved my life.'

'And Jack's.'

Selkie barked happily, remembering too.

Tristan and Edmund stared back and forth, confused.

'Where are the nearest?' Alex asked.

Nim grabbed the net and jumped to her feet. 'I'll need help to bring them back!'

She raced to the rocks at the far side of the cove.

'I guess we'll find out when we get there,' Edmund said to Tristan, and they followed her.

Selkie swam around to meet them, and Alex stayed behind with Tiffany and Ollie, watching while they slept.

On the other side of the rocks, there was a patch of white sand like a giant sandbox. It was dotted with round ball shapes, because four palm trees were growing in the sand, and the heavy rain had knocked their ripest coconuts down.

'*Revenge of the Raft!*' Edmund exclaimed. 'The Hero got the idea when a coconut nearly hit him on the head after the Bad Guys threw him off his boat!'

'We don't have time to talk about books!' Tristan shouted. 'We've got to get my sister somewhere safe!'

'That's what we're doing,' said Edmund, dumping a coconut into the net.

Nim was already halfway up the first tree. 'Watch out while I throw!'

'This is crazy,' Tristan muttered, but he started snatching up coconuts too.

Edmund dragged the net down closer to the water before it got too heavy to move. With Nim throwing coconuts down and the boys picking up, it didn't take long to fill the net.

'Twenty-seven!' Edmund counted, as he pulled the drawstring rope to close the net into a bag. Tristan helped him push it into the water, and Nim tied the end of the rope onto the strap around Selkie's shoulders.

Then, with Nim on Selkie's back and the boys on the coconut raft, they rounded the point and landed on the rocks in front of Tiffany, Ollie and Alex.

THE BREEZE WAS fresh; the first gold threads of sunset danced in the sky and the mirror of the sea. Jack's sails filled and his boat skimmed across the waves. Ahead of them the island grew steadily bigger, and the bigger it grew the more beautiful it became.

'Paradise!' exclaimed Anika and Ryan.

'Home, sweet home,' Jack started to say.

That was when he saw something that shouldn't have been there: a fast-moving shape between them and the island.

'Take the tiller!' he told Anika, as he leapt into the cabin. His satellite phone was flashing; he grabbed it too and swung back out with the binoculars to his eyes.

'Your boat's leaving!'

'It can't leave without us!' Ryan spluttered.

'The kids wouldn't do that!' Anika protested.

They stopped when Jack read his message aloud:

Tiffany is stuck in a shaft in a cave. Edmund with her. Leonora and Lance trying to steal fossil. Nim gone to ask them for help; doesn't know they are truly evil. I'm heading back to cave with Tristan and Ollie. PLEASE COME HOME FAST AS YOU CAN. Alex.

The time on the message was an hour and a half ago.

Jack pulled the extra sail out of its bag and rigged it to the top of the mast with the first. He tugged it out to the other side so that the two sails flew out like a frigate bird's wings, catching every single breath of wind. The boat flew faster than it had ever sailed before.

THE COCONUT RAFT had just enough room for Alex and Tiffany to hold Ollie between them, and the boys to rest on the back and kick. Nim wanted to swim, but Selkie barked *NO!* because the rocks were sharp and the waves were rough on this side of the island. So she rode on Selkie's back, which was what she liked doing best in all the world, except when they were towing five people, and one of those people was injured and another was a baby.

Selkie swam steadily the length of the Black Rocks, on past the steam drifting from the Hissing Stones and the jagged curve of Keyhole Cove. Now the waves were gentler and the water was a lighter, brighter blue. They passed the other sea lions basking in the sun. Soon Selkie would turn to weave her way through the maze of coral reef, and they would all be safe.

A deep rumble roared over the waves. The fishing boat crashed out through the reef. Leonora was steering with Lance behind her shouting instructions. They'd been back to the camp to get the rest of their things from the tent – and now they were heading straight for the raft.

'Hang on!' Nim screamed over her shoulder.

She clung tight to Selkie. The boat swerved so close that just before the wave swamped her, Nim saw the rage on Leonora's face. *She's not beautiful at all!* Nim thought, but then she was swept off Selkie, gasping and somersaulting, and couldn't think about anything except getting back to the air.

She popped up beside the raft, ready to dive again. The boat's wake was so violent she was sure Ollie would have fallen off.

'Whee!' shouted the little boy. 'Can we do it again?'

Nim hoped he'd like it as much the second time. The boat was circling in a wide, wild loop and powering back towards them.

JACK POINTED THE sailboat tight into the wind, begging her for every bit of speed she had.

'Maybe Tris and Alex are taking it to rescue Tiff,' Anika said, but she didn't believe it any more than Jack or Ryan did. How would they use a boat to get someone out of a tunnel?

As they watched through the binoculars, the boat turned, and then disappeared around Sea Lion Point.

'Could the message be a joke?' Ryan asked.

'Alex Rover doesn't joke about evil,' said Jack. He hadn't meant to say 'Alex Rover', he'd meant just to say 'Alex', but instead the whole line had slipped out. Nim had read it in a book review and they'd all thought it was so funny that it had become a regular saying between them.

It wasn't funny now, though. He could see the look on Anika and Ryan's faces: *Is he crazy?*

'Alex lives on the island with us,' Jack explained, blushing a little. 'She didn't want anyone to know. She wouldn't have sent that message unless the danger was real.'

They were close enough now to see Shell Beach – but there was no boat in sight.

'I don't care about our boat!' Anika exclaimed. 'I just want to get to Tiffany.'

'Where do you think the tunnel is?' asked Ryan.

'We'll start near the Emergency Cave,' said Jack. He pushed the tiller hard over to tack; the sails flapped as Ryan and Anika pulled them across to the other side. The sailboat settled onto her new course, sea foam flying over her deck.

They saw the Lowes' boat a minute later. It was stuck fast on Sea Lion Point on the edge of Keyhole Cove.

Jack steered the sailboat ever faster, until they were close enough to see Leonora and Lance on the deck and the angry sea lions milling around them. Ryan and Anika pulled down the extra sail and the sailboat slowed obediently.

'WHERE ARE OUR KIDS?'

Leonora and Lance stared straight ahead and didn't answer.

'Keep on heading this direction and stay well out from the rocks,' Jack said, and jumped over the side.

'You steer,' said Ryan to Anika, and dived in after Jack.

He hadn't swum four strokes when Anika shouted, 'There they are!'

Jack and Ryan turned and swam back so fast that the water churned. They reached the raft just as the sack of coconuts bumped against the sailboat's side.

Alex and Edmund lifted Ollie up to Anika. Then it was Tiffany's turn. With Ryan and Tristan pushing from the raft, and her mother pulling from the deck, somehow she slid up onto the sailboat without bumping her swollen foot.

Tristan and Edmund followed.

Nim cut the raft-rope from around Selkie's shoulders, and Jack tied it to the stern of his sailboat. He hugged Nim quickly as they trod water. 'Hop up on the boat with the other kids. The tide's coming in, and I need to sort out Leonora and Lance before the boat floats off the rocks.'

Alex slipped off the raft into the water beside him, and Ryan was waiting on the other side.

'I'm coming too!' Nim shouted.

'You're too tired,' said Alex.

'You're too angry,' said Jack, and that was the truth. Nim was so angry she could have skipped across the water without touching the surface. *You hurt our island!* she wanted to scream. *You made me blow up the beautiful fossil; you tried to kill the bats; you didn't care if you killed Tiffany ... and now you tried to drown us all. I can't believe I trusted you!*

In a terrible, shameful way, the last thing hurt worst of all. It was the only thing she could have changed, and if she'd changed it, everything else would have been different too. If she hadn't thought Leonora was so beautiful and clever; if she hadn't wanted to please her and show off to the other kids; if she hadn't been so sure that Leonora couldn't possibly be as bad as Tiffany said, then the fossil might still be there and none of the other things would have happened at all.

She wanted to get close enough to Leonora and Lance to pinch like a crab, bite like a shark, sting like a bee.

'I'll stay back with Selkie,' she promised.

Jack knew that Selkie wouldn't let Nim get into danger. 'Okay,' he said.

So, with Nim riding beside them, Jack, Alex and Ryan swam towards the stranded boat. Alex wasn't a strong swimmer, but Selkie stayed close.

Behind them, the other sea lions fanned out in a honking, splashing army.

And behind that, the sailboat looped in wide, lazy circles. Tristan loosened the sails so that only the vaguest puffs of wind stayed in them, just enough that Edmund could steer while Anika looked after her wounded daughter.

There was nowhere for Leonora and Lance to go. Their faces twisted with rage, but they didn't try to fight when Jack and Alex leapt on board, not even when Alex tripped and nearly skidded across the deck into them. They watched as Ryan checked the boat for damage, then pushed it off the rocks and climbed on board too. They didn't speak when he started the motor and drove a little further out from the rocks.

All the while, Nim stayed on Selkie's back, watching but saying nothing.

Then, when Ryan cut the engine and Jack let down the anchor in the middle of the honking, barking sea lion army, Lance finally asked, 'Where are we going?'

'You're not going anywhere for now,' said Jack. 'Selkie's friends will see to that.'

'We're going back to check the kids' injuries,' said Alex, and she glared at them so fiercely that Lance sat down hard and Leonora stepped back, forgetting that she was already standing against the rail. Her foot slipped out, she waved her arms to balance, and flipped backwards over the side.

The sea lions surrounded her, whuffling curiously. Leonora screamed as if she were being attacked by sharks. Her arms and legs thrashed, she gulped in water each time she screamed, and with every gulp she bobbed a little lower.

Nim could still feel her anger bubbling, lava-hot.

'Come on, Selkie,' she said.

Selkie pushed her way through the other sea lions. Nim slid off. With a mighty shove, she pushed Leonora across Selkie's back. Ryan and Jack grabbed the struggling woman's arms and hauled her back on board like a hooked fish, while Lance sat still, staring into space.

Leonora stayed where she'd plonked onto the deck, dripping and bedraggled. She didn't speak.

And just like that, Nim's rage washed away. She didn't ever want to see the Bijous again, and she would never forget the terrible things they'd done. But these miserable, defeated people couldn't go on making her feel as if she was going to explode.

'Selkie,' she said, 'ask your friends to let us pass. But make sure Lance and Leonora stay right where they are!'

Selkie barked sharply; some of the other sea lions barked back. Leonora shuddered. Ryan took the boat keys out of the ignition and dropped them safely in his pocket.

Then Jack, Alex and Ryan dived overboard and swam through the crowd of honking animals back to the sailboat.

As Jack took the tiller again to circle for home, Selkie flopped up onto the coconut raft. The other sea lions watched as she rode, honking happily, back to Shell Beach.

THEY ALL WENT up to the house together. Tiffany rode on her father's back, and Ollie wanted his mum to piggyback him too. There was a lot to tell, and they had to keep stopping because everyone was talking at once and asking questions, and the parents were wiping their eyes and getting angry as they listened … but the first thing was to check Tiffany's wound. Her foot was swollen, bruised and bloody, but Anika didn't think anything was broken.

She cleaned and bandaged it again, and then made the rest of them line up to check all the scratches and cuts that they'd been too busy to notice.

'What about that cramp in your other foot?' Edmund asked Tiffany.

'It was okay as soon as I put it in the hot water,' said Tiffany.

'Hot water?' Jack asked,

'The water in the bat cave was hot,' Edmund explained.

'And thick and slimy,' said Tiffany.

'Like algae sludge,' said Edmund.

'That's what the water in the side tunnel was like too,' Nim said slowly. 'But it didn't get hot until I dropped Tiffany's sneaker in it.'

'There was no algae in my sneaker!' Tiffany protested.

'But it was full of coconut oil, and the puddle was full of algae,' said Nim. 'When they mixed together, the water heated up so fast it was fizzing.'

'The puddle started fizzing when I put my foot in, too!' said Tiffany.

'I tried to find a test tube in Lance and Leonora's tool bag,' said Nim. 'They didn't have one.'

'I did,' said Tiffany, and pulled her water bottle out of its pouch on her belt.

It was just a plain plastic drink bottle, but they all stared at it as if it were the most precious jewel in the universe.

'What's that?' asked Ollie.

'It might be the biofuel that saves the world,' said Jack.

'Oh,' said Ollie.

'An algae that lives in stagnant water,' said Ryan, 'and reacts with coconut oil.'

'Let's not get our hopes up,' said Anika.

'Why not?' asked Nim, because whatever happened in the end, it was always much more fun to hope.

Chapter 16

From: Tiffany@kidmail.com
To: Nim@RusoeSanctuaryforRare&EndangeredSpecies.com
Date: Friday, 27 June, 10:05am
Subject: Crutches

Hi Nim

I never knew how beautiful your island was until we were going home. I sat on the deck watching until I couldn't see it anymore and Mum made me have a rest in the cabin.

Mum took me to the hospital as soon as we landed. The doctor said my ankle is badly sprained and I have to use crutches and wear a big boot for a few weeks. I don't think she believed me when I told her how it happened, especially when I said about Selkie carrying me out of the rainforest. She told Mum that I should stay in hospital for a while because I was confused. Mum said it was much better than how I was normally. Anyway, in the end she let Mum bring me home.

Please give Selkie a big hug for me.

Your friend

Tiffany

From: Tris@kidmail.com
To: Nim@RusoeSanctuaryforRare&EndangeredSpecies.com,
Edmund@kidmail.com
Date: Friday, 27 June, 10:15am
Subject: Tiff on crutches

Hi Nim, hi Edmund

Tiff wouldn't let me take a picture of her on crutches because she says the boot makes her look like Bigfoot, but Ollie drew this one for you.

Thanks for saving my sister.

Tris

From: Edmund@kidmail.com
To: Nim@RusoeSanctuaryforRare&EndangeredSpecies.com
Date: Friday, 27 June, 10:15am
Subject: Hi to Fred

Hi Nim

It feels very weird being home. No sea lions, iguanas, crazy adventure girls, cliffs, caves or explosions. But at least I'm not grounded this time.

My mum took me to see Selina Ashburn on the way home. She looks like a ghost but she got so mad when she heard what Lance and Leonora did that she said she didn't have time to throw up anymore. Luckily she'd saved a piece of the cake L & L made them. She's sent it to the lab to see if it's been poisoned. (I BET it has!)

When I told her about the algae she phoned Peter Hunterstone and he got straight into a taxi and came over too. They can't wait to start testing and experimenting on the sample.

Edmund – missing the island as much as Fred would miss Nim

From: Edmund@kidmail.com
To: Nim@RusoeSanctuaryforRare&EndangeredSpecies.com, Tiffany@kidmail.com, Tris@kidmail.com
Date: Friday, 27 June, 10:18am
Subject: Fossil Pictures

These turned out even better than I expected. It's sad it's gone but at least we have proof that it was real.

Edmund

From: Nim@RusoeSanctuaryforRare&EndangeredSpecies.com
To: Edmund@kidmail.com, Tiffany@kidmail.com, Tris@kidmail.com
Date: Friday, 27 June, 11:25am
Subject: Super Algae and Super Friends

Hi everyone,

I've never had three emails all at once! Tiffany, I'm really glad your ankle is going to be okay and that you didn't have to stay in hospital.

Tris, please tell Ollie I loved his picture.

Edmund, those pictures are fantastic! Now we know we're not crazy. Or maybe a little bit crazy, but at least we didn't make up the fossil of Chica's great-great-grandmother.

That's good Selina and Peter are getting better. I wonder if it really was poison?

The island seems quiet now you've gone.

You know when Jack and Ryan took Lance and Leonora off your boat so you could leave? The Coast Guard got here a few hours later and took them away. I wished they didn't have to be on the island even for that long, but Selkie sat in their tent doorway so they didn't try to escape.

We went back to the cave yesterday to get more samples of the algae. It's good there was enough in the drink bottle for you to share. Jack's started an experiment already and is writing a report of what he's discovered about the algae so far. He says he's not too excited yet but I can tell that he is.

But the best news is that Jack says that if this algae is as good as he thinks it is, everyone should come back to finish the experiments together. Except this time Edmund should come with the real Dr Ashburn and Professor Hunterstone. I guess Lance and Leonora will be in jail anyway so we won't have to worry about them.

And guess what else I found while we were collecting samples: part of Leonora's amber pendant. It must have been smashed when a rock hit it. But I can't find the scorpion anywhere.

Your friend

Nim – feeling as happy as Fred eating coconut – or Selkie scaring bad guys

P.S. Or as a scorpion free after thousands of years

P.S.S. Or as a girl with friends

about the author

WENDY ORR WAS born in Canada and spent her childhood
across Canada, France and the USA. Wherever she lived,
there were always lots of stories, books and pets.

Wendy started writing her own stories soon after
she learned to read. One story about a girl running away to live
on an island eventually led to *Nim's Island*. Another story about
adventures in caves, inspired by finding a fossilised shark's
tooth, seems to have wiggled its way into Nim's new story.

One day a film producer in Hollywood took Wendy's book
Nim's Island out of the library to read to her son. The next day
she asked if she could make it into a movie. Wendy said yes!
They became good friends, and Wendy had the fun
of helping work on the screenplay. A second film
followed, called *Return to Nim's Island*.

Wendy began writing for children after a career as an
occupational therapist. She is the author of many
award-winning books and lives on Victoria's
Mornington Peninsula.